RACHEL'S QUEST

RACHEL'S QUEST

SHEILA SPENCER-SMITH

THORNDIKE
CHIVERS

This Large Print edition is published by Thorndike Press, Waterville, Maine, USA, and by BBC Audiobooks Ltd, Bath, England.
Thorndike Press, a part of Gale, Cengage Learning.
Copyright © Sheila Spencer-Smith, 2001.
The moral right of the author has been asserted.

ALL RIGHTS RESERVED

LIBRARY OF CONGRESS CATALOGING-IN-PUBLICATION DATA

Spencer-Smith, Sheila.
    Rachel's quest / by Sheila Spencer-Smith.
        p. cm. — (Thorndike Press large print candlelight)
      ISBN-13: 978-1-4104-0586-9 (alk. paper)
      ISBN-10: 1-4104-0586-9 (alk. paper)
      1. Large type books. I. Title.
   PR6069.P487R33 2008
   823'.914—dc22   2008003473

BRITISH LIBRARY CATALOGUING-IN-PUBLICATION DATA AVAILABLE

Published in 2008 in the U.S. by arrangement with Dorian Literary Agency.
Published in 2008 in the U.K. by arrangement with the author.

U.K. Hardcover: 978 1 405 64402 0 (Chivers Large Print)
U.K. Softcover: 978 1 405 64403 7 (Camden Large Print)

Printed in the United States of America
1 2 3 4 5 6 7 12 11 10 09 08

Rachel's Quest

CHAPTER ONE

Rachel finished packing her rucksack for the most important journey of her life, and sat down on her bed. She'd included jeans, T-shirts, two pairs of trainers, night things, her thick jersey, of course, because it would be colder in the North. She was wearing her black skirt for the train, and black tights and shoes, and of course the silver cross on its chain that had meant so much to Aunt Sophie. Quickly she pushed it out of sight beneath her sweatshirt.

She took a deep, calming breath, and let it out slowly. Ticket and train timetable? Yes, both handy in the front pocket of the rucksack. There, too, was her grandmother's diary that had been the start of it all when Mr Felpham, her aunt's solicitor, had given it to her two days ago. All she had to do now was to get herself to King's Cross Station for the train to Leeds to change for Harrogate. No problem.

Standing up, she looked round the comfortable bedroom that had been hers since her aunt died. Then she pushed shut the heavy wardrobe door and straightened the lace cloth on the top of the chest of drawers. On it she placed the letter thanking Mr and Mrs Felpham for all they had done for her.

She was sorry she hadn't been awake when they returned home late last night to explain in person that Mrs Woodfield needed her at once. She left her new address, Alderbeck House, Yorkshire, deliberately vague, of course, to give her the time she needed, but with the promise to get in touch again as soon as she was settled.

She was ready now. Slinging on her jacket, and heaving up the rucksack, she opened her bedroom door. Carefully she crept down the stairs, pausing to listen for a moment in case the faint creaking of the bottom step had alerted anyone. Not a sound. Then she moved to the front door, turned the key in the lock and opened it just wide enough to squeeze herself through, pull her laden rucksack after her and then shut the door again.

Out in the fresh morning air she smiled, feeling a glow to her cheeks. She was on her way!

Safely on the train, speeding North, Rachel leaned back in her seat and closed her eyes. She hadn't slept much last night for thinking of her startling decision as she scanned the job adverts in the Enfield Gazette. She had picked up the newspaper from the doormat and carried it upstairs to read. Then she had seen Mrs Woodfield's advert with a sudden leap of her heart. With luck Mr Felpham would think she had known Mrs Woodfield for a long time, years perhaps. Surely as Aunt Sophie's solicitor he would have heard some mention of Alderbeck in the past. The subconscious was a funny thing. She was praying hard that the name would mean something to him and he would assume Mrs Woodfield was a friend of the family.

He would have been appalled had he known that she had only phoned Mrs Woodfield for the first time after the words Alderbeck House had leaped up at her from the paper spread out on her bedroom floor. She had known instantly what she wanted. She sprang up and raced down to the telephone in the hall, thankful that she was alone in the house. Mrs Woodfield's voice on the phone was reassuring as she explained that she needed someone at once as a companion-help for herself as her daughter had to be away a great deal.

"I wish to apply for the position," Rachel said. "I'm Rachel Paget, nearly twenty. I'm looking for a job. I looked after my elderly aunt for some years before she died. She was very frail so I know what's involved. I could get references."

"We're very isolated here, my dear, miles from a town of any size. Are you sure?"

"I'm sure, Mrs Woodfield. I need a new position now. At the moment I'm living with my guardians, Mr and Mrs Felpham, at twenty-seven Glebe Avenue, Enfield, London."

"Let me write that down."

The pause at the other end of the line seemed to go on for ever. Then Mrs Woodfield spoke again.

"And the phone number?"

Rachel gave it.

"My solicitor is Banks & Marple. I'll give you their phone number. Your guardians might like to know that," Mrs Woodfield went on.

"Of course."

"Why not come and stay for a few days, and we'll see how you get on? I'll reimburse you for your fare, of course. I know there's a suitable train that gets into Harrogate at about five. Someone will meet you at the station, my dear."

Hardly able to believe her luck, Rachel had put the phone down and started sorting some things out to take with her. How could she turn down a great opportunity like this? The only thing to worry about was Mr Felpham's reaction. He was strict in wishing to follow Aunt Sophie's hopes for her future that included going to university. But she didn't want that, not now. She would write to him when she got to Alderbeck and try to explain, try to get him to see how important this was to her. That way she'd have at least two days before he tried to do anything like racing North to drag her back before she'd had time to trace her grandmother's family.

Alderbeck — the place she wanted to be more than anywhere else in the world; the place where she was going to find out about the family Aunt Sophie would never talk about; the place where, already, she felt she belonged because of the diary that was tucked away inside the pocket of her rucksack.

The station platform emptied fast. Rachel pushed back her hair, and stared at the twinkling railway lines. Suppose Mrs Woodfield didn't come for her after all? Alderbeck House was miles away. The journey had been great, and her excitement had lasted until she had changed trains at Leeds. But as the local train chuntered its way towards Harrogate she felt her happy anticipation trickling away until she felt empty inside. She swallowed hard, and then picked up her rucksack and hauled it across to a seat from where she had a good view of the exit.

To fill in the waiting time she pulled the page-a-day diary from her rucksack and opened it. Warmth crept round her heart at the spidery handwriting, written so long ago by a girl only a couple of years older than herself.

And tomorrow I shall be with my dear Harry, the young Sarah Swinbank had written so long ago. *Never more to part. Dear, dear Harry, my love.*

Rachel ran a finger over the design of a rose beneath the last entry, and tried to imagine how the writer had felt as she penned these emotional words. What would she have thought if she had known the stunning effect they would have on her unknown granddaughter so many years in the future?

Mr Felpham had found the diary only the other day among her aunt's papers, and had given it to her at once.

"This will interest you, Rachel, my dear," he had said, his kind eyes twinkling at her.

"Rachel Paget?"

She leaped to her feet, dropping the diary and then picking it up quickly. A man in jeans and denim jacket was looking as if he knew her. Suddenly she felt overdressed in her dark clothes. She flushed.

"Sorry to startle you."

His blue eyes in his tanned face looked friendly.

"Simon Swinbank."

He picked up the rucksack as if it was stuffed with cotton wool.

"Mrs Woodfield asked me to pick you up, Rachel, since I had business to do in town. We'll not hang about."

She followed him outside to where a Land-Rover was parked near the station exit. Swinbank, he said his name was. Swinbank was her grandmother's surname before she married. It must be coincidence. Probably a common name round here. How often had Aunt Sophie warned her about letting her imagination run away with her? She must watch she didn't blurt out the first thing that came into her head.

He didn't speak until they left the town behind them and were speeding along a

13

straight road leading to distant purple heights.

"So you're going to be looking after Mrs Woodfield for us? That's grand."

He sounded so confident that Rachel began to relax and to look at the scenery shooting past. Rocky outcrops stood out like sentinels. Simon turned his head slightly.

"It's grand country."

She smiled at the warmth in his voice.

"My grandmother came from Yorkshire, but I've never been here before."

"Oh? So she'll have talked about it."

Rachel shook her head.

"I've only just found out. I never knew her, you see."

She expected him to ask more, but he was silent. She stared out at the villages they passed and the small town set among bare hills. A wild thrill shot through her as the narrowing road skirted sheets of water and led ever upward to rougher, craggier country. This was her grandmother's land and she was about to discover her family's roots. It meant so much to her, so very much. It was all she had now. She took a deep breath.

"I see why you love it. The lakes . . ."

"Reservoirs, they are, to serve Leeds and Bradford. The land was flooded years ago."

"Covering the fields?"

"Houses and cottages, too."

She shuddered, stupidly imagining the people drown as they went about their daily lives. Nausea rose in her so suddenly she gulped. Glancing at her, Simon slowed down and drew into a lay-by.

"Like a closer look? It won't hurt to get a breath of air."

She opened the door and stumbled out. Her gasping breath brought tears to her eyes. It was heady stuff, this moorland air that smelled of peat and water and mountain tops. In silence he handed her a folded white handkerchief.

"Better now?"

She nodded, wiping her eyes. He was really kind. She felt she had found a friend already and was pleased.

"The people were re-housed," he said. "Water is one of the necessities of life. There has to be enough for those in the cities."

They got back into the Land-Rover. Soon they would be at Alderbeck House and she would meet Mrs Woodfield, her employer. She thought suddenly of the job she had come to do. Up to now there hadn't been much time to wonder how she would cope. Suppose Mrs Woodfield thought she was too young to be a companion to her after all and she was sent straight back?

Alderbeck House, square-fronted and grey, stood well back from the road among lawns and dark conifers. Someone had been tending the daffodils near the front door, and a garden fork was stuck in the ground nearby. The tyres crunched across the gravel. Rachel's breath was tight in her throat as they got out of the Land-Rover. The door of the house opened immediately and a slim, grey-haired lady came down the steps to greet them. Mrs Woodfield, of course.

"Oh, Simon, thank goodness you've come," she said quickly. "Rachel, my dear."

Her voice shook.

"Celia, what's wrong?" Simon asked.

"It was just after you phoned."

Mrs Woodfield raised a hand and seemed to clutch at the air.

"I couldn't reach you. Nerissa wants you. She's admitted herself to the nursing home. It's been such a shock. I've been praying that you would come soon."

Rachel sprang forward at the same time as Simon, and together they caught her as she slumped forward. They lowered her gently to the step where she sat leaning on Simon, her eyes closed and her face ashen. Rachel, utterly helpless, stared in dismay. Then Mrs Woodfield stirred and struggled to her feet in spite of Simon's restraining hand.

"Wait a minute. Give yourself time," he said gruffly.

"I'm all right now."

She smiled slightly at Rachel.

"What a welcome for you, my dear. Julie, our housekeeper, will look after you while Simon and I are gone. Oh, yes, Simon, I'm coming with you to the nursing home, this instant."

Rachel was surprised he didn't argue as he escorted her down the steps to the Land-Rover. She watched them drive away, and then went into the house and closed the door. A wave of loneliness swept over her as she thought of the precious diary and her rucksack left in the Land-Rover. Then she went to investigate the door at the end of the silent hall.

She found herself in the sitting-room, a long room with flowered sofa and arm-chairs. Near the window stood a music stand and nearby was a violin case leaning against the wall. A sound in the doorway made her swing round, and she saw a rather plump girl in a jersey and skirt smiling at her.

"I'm Julie Hepinstall," she said, "and you're Rachel, the companion-help. I'm the housekeeper. Fancy a cup of tea in the kitchen? I've a pot made."

In the kitchen doorway, Rachel stood and blinked at the bright colours. Julie gave another rich laugh.

"Takes you by surprise, doesn't it? Cheering on a dull day, any road."

She pulled a stool out from under the table.

"Sit you down. Dinner's been put back a bit."

"But what's happened?" Rachel asked. "I mean, they've gone to a nursing home, haven't they, and I wondered . . . I mean, who's Nerissa?"

"They've not said owt to me, but they're worried, you can see that," Julie said. "Poor Mrs Woodfield. Nerissa's her daughter. Best thing for her, back in the nursing home. They'll soon sort her out and a good thing, too. She's been nuisance enough to her mother here the last few weeks."

Rachel looked at her in surprise. Julie had sounded sympathetic a moment ago until the mention of Nerissa changed the expression on her face. But then Julie smiled again as she placed the milk jug on the table and then sat down heavily on her stool with the large teapot in front of her.

"Will you settle all right here at Alderbeck, Rachel?" she asked as she started to pour. "It's right lonely."

Rachel smiled, pushing the thought of Nerissa to the back of her mind.

"I'm used to being on my own. My aunt was ill for a long time, before she died. I looked after her quite a bit, so I didn't go out much."

"You lived with her?"

"She brought me up. I don't remember my parents at all."

"Died, did they?"

"In a plane crash in France, when I was a baby."

The sympathy in Julie's eyes was unnerving, and Rachel looked quickly down at her cup of tea that was too hot to drink.

"And you, Julie?" she asked, looking up again. "Have you always lived round here?"

"Aye, born and bred. We got the cottage to live in when we were wed. My husband got the job as gardener here, you see."

Rachel took a gulp of tea.

"It was kind of Simon Swinbank to come all the way to the station to meet me. Who is he, Julie?"

"Great friends they've always been, Wood-fields and Swinbanks," Julie said. "He was nobbut a lad when his folks died and he took over the farm. He's made a grand job of it and he not yet twenty-seven."

Rachel considered. Simon looked younger than that in spite of his serious demeanour. In her mind's eye she saw the way his eyes crinkled when he smiled that slow smile she was already beginning to find attractive. She liked the way a lock of his wavy hair kept falling over his forehead each time he turned his head.

"Is he married, Julie?"

Julie shook her head.

"Not any more. He was too young to be wed and it didn't last long. He's well rid though it's lonely for him up there on the moor."

Rachel had noticed a fleeting, sad expression in his eyes. She tucked the memory away in her mind to bring out later to think about.

"Do you know a place round here called Alderbeck Court?" she asked suddenly.

"This is Alderbeck House, but I've not heard tell of owt other. Alderbeck Court?"

Rachel nodded. Should she tell Julie why she had come? No, she'd think she was crazy, coming all the way here because of an entry in an old diary. She would have to find Alderbeck Court for herself.

The telephone rang in the hall. Julie swung one sturdy leg over the other as she got up to answer it.

"You stay right where you are, Rachel," she said when she came back. "That was Simon from Rawthwaite Nursing Home. They're bringing Nerissa home now, if you please. She's discharged herself. I thought she would. She's like that, causing a right upheaval to get her own way."

Julie frowned as she collected the cups and saucers and carried them to the sink.

"I'll need to set a tray for Nerissa. She'll eat in her room. I'm to set yours and Mrs Woodfield's in't dining-room."

Rachel watched her strain vegetables and whip cream. In hardly anytime at all she heard sounds of arrival outside. She stayed where she was, listening to Julie's deep voice in the hall as she went out to greet them. There were other voices, more subdued, and the sound of doors opening and closing. What was happening out there? When Julie came back she looked serious.

"Mrs Woodfield'll be ready to see you in a minute. Best wait in the dining-room. I'll take the soup in now."

To Rachel's dismay, Simon left almost at once. He was a familiar figure and without his presence she felt lonely. There was something about his grey eyes and his slow smile she found reassuring even though they had only just met.

Before Mrs Woodfield joined her Rachel pulled her skirt straight, and pushed her loose hair behind her ears. She wished now she had tied it back in the hope she would look older. She knew that there was another reason now for her wishing to remain here as well as finding out about her family. She had never met anyone like Simon Swinbank before. Once or twice she had become friendly with boys from school but she had never been remotely interested in them in the way she was already beginning to think of this man whom she had only just met. It was a disquieting thought that she might not have the chance to get to know him better.

Mrs Woodfield smiled kindly at her as they seated themselves, one on either side of the large table in the room whose windows looked over the dusky front garden. With her mind obviously on her daughter upstairs, she spoke little as they began to eat.

"Forgive me, my dear," she said as they finished the meal and Julie brought in the coffee. "We're not usually like this. I can't say more now. Thank goodness my daughter's home now, perhaps for good."

"For good?"

"I'd like to think so."

Mrs Woodfield poured coffee for them both.

"We'll talk more about it tomorrow, Rachel, and Nerissa will want to see you."

Rachel's hand shook a little as she picked up her cup. A threat? Of course not. But she wished it didn't sound like one.

Chapter Two

Next morning Rachel woke early, tense with anticipation. Her bedroom seemed larger than it had yesterday evening when she had lugged her rucksack upstairs and unpacked her few belongings. Someone had placed fluffy towels and a container of talcum powder for her use in the ensuite shower room.

Suddenly it was too much. She wanted to be outside, starting the search while she had the chance. She threw on jeans, T-shirt and her thick jersey and trainers. Pulling a comb through her hair, she opened the bedroom door, and crept down the wide staircase and out of the unlocked front door.

There was no-one about. She paused for a moment to sniff the murky air, expecting to smell the peaty scent of open moorland. It smelled only of cold that whipped glowingly against her cheeks.

From the gravel drive an inviting path led across grass to a gate into the churchyard beyond — a good place to do a bit of detective work. She started by examining the headstones, moving slowly between them in the long, damp grass until the legs of her jeans were soaked to her knees. Then she went to the church door, and finding it unlocked pushed it open and went inside.

For a moment she could see nothing, and she wrinkled her nose at the mouldy smell. Then she wandered up and down gazing at the memorial tablets on the walls. The writing on most of them was hard to make out in the gloom, but she could see enough to realise there was no mention of her grandmother's family name. Perhaps she had missed something.

She looked round for light switches, and found them hidden by the curtain by the door. Blinking in the glare, she could see at once there were no more tablets. She looked hopefully at the table containing various leaflets, and opened the visitor's book to flip through for some clue.

Amazing to think that in this church in which the family of the young Sarah Swinbank would surely have worshipped, there was no obvious sign that they had ever lived nearby. Disappointment welled up in her.

Alderbeck Court had to be in the district somewhere. Simon Swinbank would know. Next time she saw him she would ask. She should have done so before.

Light reflected brilliantly on the windows with their coloured pictures in stained glass. With a last look round she left the church, plunging it into gloom again as she switched off the lights and closed the heavy door behind her. Surely it was darker out here now? A rumble in the distance made her shiver. Thunder? She hated thunder.

Head down, she ran along the path to the gate, and then stopped. Ahead of her was an upright tomb, like a box. One side was smashed in, and the stone on the top looked as if it would slide off at a touch. Her heart lurched to see it so suddenly. The wind and rain had done this over a long period of time. Whose tomb was it? She looked close.

When a twig snapped behind her, she spun round, her hand to her mouth, to see a dark-haired man in jeans and red-checked shirt.

"What do you want?" she gasped.

"You've found your way out here, any road."

She took a step back.

"Who are you?"

His bold eyes laughed down into hers.

"So it were you who put the lights on in't church? I thought I'd left them on myself. That's all right then. No harm done."

"I had a look round," Rachel said, struggling to keep calm. "I'd better get back before it rains."

He laughed but didn't move to let her pass.

"I saw you looking at my great grandad's tomb. A fine lad, old Zachary, as wild as they come so they've always said."

"Excuse me, please."

"Nowt's amiss, surely? A pretty lass like you needs company."

To her relief he moved to one side, but then decided to accompany her. Although he was wearing heavy boots he had crept up on her across the grass without a sound. Now, on the gravel path, she was conscious of his footsteps.

The rain came as they reached the gate, bucketing down from a black sky and soaking her in seconds. She didn't see him go, but she was on her own as she burst through the kitchen door. Trembling, she stood for a moment, letting the water drip off her on to Julie's clean floor. She peeled off her wet jersey, and slipped her feet out of her trainers. There was no sign of Julie. She reached for a hand towel and rubbed her hair hard.

Then she went into the hall where a grateful warmth met her. The radiators were comfortably hot as she rested her hands on them. If only her aunt could have enjoyed some of the comforts provided here.

A sound from above made her look up. Mrs Woodfield leaned over the banisters on the landing.

"Oh, there you are, Rachel, my dear. Will you come up? Nerissa would like to see you now. My dear, are you all right?"

Rachel hesitated. Then she took the stairs two at a time, and arrived at the top with flushed cheeks and pounding heart.

"I'm a bit wet," she said, pushing her damp hair behind her ears and trying to keep the quiver from her voice. "I went out. I won't take long to change."

Mrs Woodfield seemed not to notice Rachel's bedraggled appearance. She looked down at the red roses she was carrying.

"Aren't they lovely? They've just arrived. Julie left them on the landing table. Nerissa won't keep you long. Just a quick word, that's all."

Rachel nodded, and followed Mrs Woodfield along the passage and into the room at the end. She looked in amazement at Nerissa who lay on the bed in a gold and crimson dressing-gown with her dark hair loose about her face. Red velvet curtains cut out most of the light, but she could see enough to imagine herself on the set of one of the television plays Aunt Sophie liked so much. It was the strangest feeling. For a moment she thought she could step straight out of it into her aunt's familiar room and be back in her old life instead of here among strangers. Then she blinked, remembering.

Nerissa took the roses from her mother, and opened the attached card.

"Brian!" she said scornfully. "Where did he get these?"

"Not from the garden in March," Mrs Woodfield said so tartly that Rachel giggled.

Then, remembering the real situation, she looked at Nerissa in sympathy. Nerissa frowned.

"So Brian's been off to Rawthwaite again?"

"As long as he wanders off in his own time who am I to query it?"

For a moment her daughter looked annoyed, as if she needed to get to the bottom of something important. Rachel stared at Nerissa in surprise. What could it possibly matter to her to make her look like that?

Suddenly Nerissa's face softened, and she held the roses to her face. Then she threw them from her and turned to Rachel for the first time. Her speculative glance travelled from her head to her feet.

"So, you're here to help out with my mother, are you?"

Rachel smiled anxiously, aware of her clinging wet clothes and straggly hair.

"Rachel's a good girl," Mrs Woodfield said. "I've told her we're not usually at sixes and sevens like this. I hope we'll soon be able to get ourselves into a sensible routine."

Nerissa moved a little on the soft bed.

"As long as you don't expect me to be bothered."

She nodded at Rachel in dismissal.

"You can take my tray down to the kitchen now."

Rachel escaped thankfully, and paused on the landing to get her breath back. She had never met anyone quite like Nerissa before. What had she let herself in for? For a second she wished herself back in the Felphams' house where everything was normal. Then she gave herself a little shake, and went downstairs to the kitchen.

She heard voices as she approached. Turning the handle, she pushed the door open with one shoulder and carried the tray inside. Julie came forward to take it from her. Her cheeks were flushed and her eyes bright. Horrified, Rachel recognised the dark-haired man from the churchyard whose bold eyes had made her want to run away from him as fast as she could. He had changed now into dry jeans and another checked shirt. He leaned against one of the bright units, and grinned at her.

"So, lass, we meet again! Julie wanted to know where you'd got to."

"With Mrs Woodfield and Nerissa, upstairs."

"In them wet clothes?"

"Leave her be!" Julie cried.

He frowned as he turned his attention to her.

"You'll get more of what I gave you earlier, lass, if you're not careful. So think on."

His dark eyes were full of contempt as he moved to the open door and paused with his hand on the handle. Then he went through, crashing it shut behind him. Julie unpacked the tray.

"Take no notice, Rachel. He's harmless, is Brian."

Harmless! Rachel couldn't speak. Brian before made her feel tainted, as if everything was somehow her fault. Julie's eyes were sparkling blue as she smiled at her.

"I'll make us a hot drink while you get out of them wet things, Rachel. Mrs Woodfield's had breakfast so I'll lay yours in here. I'll not take long."

"But who is he?"

"Brian? He's my man. Don't worry about Brian. He'll not bother you, Rachel."

No way! She'd make quite sure of that. So it was Julie's husband who had sent Nerissa red roses? What on earth had she let herself in for, coming to live and work at Alderbeck? Something was badly wrong. Rachel felt it in the air when Mrs Woodfield came downstairs to have a few words with Julie. She left them in the kitchen together, feeling that what they had to say to each other might be private.

In the large, gloomy hall the light from the fanlight above the front door illuminated the carved wooden panel on the wall above the telephone. For a moment Rachel had the strangest feeling that she was looking at something copied from a tombstone, but when she went closer she could see at once that it was nothing of the sort. Someone had carved an intricate tree design. She looked at it with pleasure for a moment or two before the kitchen door opened and Mrs Woodfield emerged. She called to Rachel to come with her into the sitting-room.

"Rachel, my dear," she said as they sat down together on the sofa, "I feel I owe you an explanation about what's been happening since your arrival. I was meaning to phone your guardian, too, but perhaps that won't be necessary now after all."

Rachel's throat felt dry.

"Not necessary?"

"Don't look so worried, my dear."

Mrs Woodfield leaned forward and patted Rachel's cold hand.

"I meant, of course, that Nerissa won't be leaving for the foreseeable future. She's been rather ill, you see, though she thinks she's better than she is. Anyway she's agreed to stay on for the next few months. You're welcome to stay here as a holiday of course, Rachel, until we decide what to do for the best. We're not throwing you out. Don't think that, my dear. And now I must get back to Nerissa."

For a moment Rachel stood looking after her, feeling empty inside. Was Mrs Woodfield trying to break it gently to her that she was no longer required because Nerissa would be here to look after her instead?

In the kitchen Julia was unloading the dishwasher. She straightened and spun round.

"I know all't time something like this would happen. It's all Nerissa's doing. She's like that, is Nerissa. Can't bear anyone to make arrangements but herself."

She sank down on a stool by the table and stared at Rachel, breathing deeply.

"Aye, this is right bad for you. It would have been grand having you here, Rachel. Just as we were getting to know one another, too. I'm right sorry."

Rachel nodded. Mrs Woodfield, kind though she was, wanted her out. Maybe she could find some other employment in the area and somewhere to live. For a moment she felt hopeful, but then reality struck. In this deserted place? But she wouldn't give up. She would think of something to keep her here, not only to pursue her quest but also to be near Simon.

There was the sound of scraping feet outside, and Brian came in. He looked at Rachel, but stood behind Julie and put one arm round her shoulder. She shrugged it off.

"Give over, Brian. I've all't rooms to do."

"The old lady's a right slave driver."

His bright eyes seemed to invite Rachel to share the joke. She flushed, and looked away quickly.

"There's nowt for you here, my lad," Julie cried. "Get off back to your digging."

Before he could move Rachel was out of the kitchen. She wasn't used to all this clamour, all these people. She needed time on her own to think. Grabbing her jacket from the hall cupboard, she rushed outside. She felt the biting wind bring colour to her cheeks as she ran up the track to the high ground behind the house. Over the brow she sank down, breathing hard, and gazed at the bleak moorland that stretched as far as she could see. A dark line of wall traversed the whole scene like a rope on a mottled blanket.

The only sound was the faint bleat of a distant sheep. It was great. Already this wild country was getting into her blood. Her warm feeling of belonging lasted only until she remembered that unless she could find herself another job and accommodation very soon there wouldn't be time to find any clues about the location of Alderbeck Court. Apart from the name there was nothing in the diary about it, not even a description of the house.

She sighed, thinking of her aunt. Had she read her mother's diary, or had it been hidden away, forgotten, until Mr Felpham unearthed it? Impossible to think that Sarah Swinbank's daughter wouldn't have been curious about her mother's young life in this beautiful, wild place. Or had Sarah never talked about it, put it out of her mind

34

for ever as soon as she and Harry were married and started their new life? Even so it was odd.

Where the ground began to slope downwards ahead of her Rachel saw a line of something darker, and sprang up to investigate. The ground away from the track was soggy, and she had to take care to jump from one tuft of heather to the next. Now she was closer she could see that the mounds like giant beehives were made from stones and heather. They were hides for men with guns. She had heard of shooting moors. This must be one of them.

She leaned back against one of them and looked round her, liking the feeling of space and height. If only she didn't have to go away from all this. How could she bear it?

With Nerissa available now to look after her mother she couldn't stay at Alderbeck. She really would have to start looking round for something. Taking a deep breath of peaty air, Rachel struggled to push her worries to the back of her mind, but how could she stop thinking about them when the house seemed to be full of suffocating sadness?

There was some sort of path a little way from her, and she started moving towards it on the firmest ground she could find. Suddenly a brown bird shot up from her feet.

She let out a startled yell, and then smiled, shamefaced. What did it matter what noise she made when there was no-one within miles?

The path widened into a track farther down, and she could see that it joined another one in the distance that would take her back to Alderbeck House. Confidently she leaped ahead, only to find herself knee deep in slimy mud. She pulled one foot out with a squelch, over-balanced and fell headlong. As she got herself up and back on the path she saw a vehicle on the track ahead. Spluttering and rubbing her face, she looked down at her clothes covered in black mud. Yanking up some dead bracken she tried to scrub the worst of it off without making much difference.

The vehicle, a Land-Rover, she could now see, pulled to a halt and to her relief she saw Simon Swinbank leap out followed by a black and white dog.

"In trouble?" he called.

No need to answer, only to get to him quickly.

"You'd better jump in," he said, taking one look at her.

"I fell in the mud. I'd better walk."

"We're not afraid of a bit of mess, are we, Fly?"

The dog licked her hand. She saw that Simon's cords were far from spotless and he wore heavy rubber boots. She climbed up into the Land-Rover, and he shut the door behind her and went round to his side. Fly leaped into the back, and stood behind Rachel with his hot, panting breath on the back of her neck. She kept her muddy feet together, trying not to spread mud everywhere.

"My trainers aren't right for this," she said as they set off down the uneven track.

"You need hiking boots. Something strong enough to support your ankles. There's a place down in Rawthwaite that could fit you out."

Simon was talking as if she was settled here for good, but at the best she had only a day or two more. She tried not to think about it as she slipped her jacket off and folded it inside out on her knee.

"Dare I ask if you've been enjoying yourself?" Simon asked.

She looked at him sharply, and saw the same sadness in his face she had noticed yesterday. Surely he didn't imagine she didn't care about having to leave? She was losing her hoped-for job for a start, apart from anything else.

"It's great," she said. "But some massive

37

bird shot up at my feet."

"You'll have put up a grouse."

"The colours everywhere are terrific. All those browns and yellows."

He nodded.

"I've been up here with bales for the sheep. The work had to be done, but it's a sad time. I'll be glad when all this worry with Nerissa is over. My mother-in-law has been through a lot lately."

Rachel was startled.

"Mother-in-law?"

"Ex-mother-in-law, Mrs Woodfield. Nerissa and I were once married."

Married to Nerissa! Rachel's sudden jolt of pain surprised her. The glamorous Nerissa and Simon, so quiet and serious, seemed so unsuited. Had Nerissa hurt him badly before they split up? It was easy to believe she had. Maybe that was the cause of his momentary sadness. Could he still be in love with her?

They arrived back at the entrance to Alderbeck House and Simon drove with care through the gateway, pulling up outside the front door. He turned to smile at her.

"It's fortunate you're here, Rachel. You'll keep Mrs Woodfield company and she'll like that."

"But I won't be needed now. Nerissa's

staying on."

"She is?"

Was it her imagination or did his mouth soften for an instant? She couldn't be sure. In any case why should it matter to her?

"That's what Mrs Woodfield said."

"Aye, so you're worried you'll be sent packing, eh? I'd better look into it when I come back later. Meanwhile, do what you can."

He gave her a warm smile.

"Of course, I will," she murmured as she opened the door of the Land-Rover.

The muscles of her legs ached as she jumped out. Her heart ached, too, as she watched the Land-Rover drive away.

CHAPTER THREE

Rachel heard music being played as she walked through the hall to breakfast next morning. Suddenly it stopped. She opened the sitting-room door, and was surprised to see Nerissa at the music stand with a violin in one hand. Her dark hair was tied back from her face which looked pale in the light from the window.

"What do you want?" Nerissa said without turning round.

Before Rachel could answer she raised the

instrument, picked up her bow and began to play. The sound was like a rippling stream of water. When it came to an end Rachel let out the breath she had been holding.

"Mother's got this bad heart. Back trouble, too," Nerissa said abruptly. "She needs someone here in the house to do a few things for her. I'll list the duties for you."

Placing the violin and bow on the table at her side, she paced the length of the room and back again to the window. Her shoulders were hunched, and her back, in her dark dress, looked hostile. Rachel opened her mouth to speak, and then closed it again. A surge of hope ran through her. What did this mean? Was she needed here after all?

Then Nerissa picked up her violin once more, and the shrieking sound that now came from it made Rachel wince. Gone was the soft music that had charmed her before. She thought suddenly of Simon Swinbank in his working clothes up on the moor seeing to his sheep. If only she could see his wind-tanned face again now and listen to his quiet voice telling her about this land he loved so much. He gave a touch of normality to things.

She escaped to the empty kitchen where breakfast was laid for her, glad to be alone.

There was a lot to think about. If Mrs Woodfield wanted her to stay on she would, no question of that, but Nerissa disliked her. Why? And why was she needed here anyway with Nerissa here, and Julie to look after things?

She ate cereal and toast, deep in thought. This was where she wanted to be, needed to be. Finding her roots was important. Mr Felpham must understand that. Maybe she'd phone him later. She thought of him picking up the phone in the gloomy hall and listening with his head held to one side as he gave deep consideration to her plans. He always did this with anything put before him, looking as if he thought the other person was trying to catch him out. Then, when he had made up his mind whether they were or not, he would smile and reply to them politely.

It had long been her aunt's hope that Rachel should go on to university. She seemed to hear his voice in her mind reminding her of this, but it was her future, wasn't it? What could be more important than discovering you weren't alone in the world after all, that somewhere you had a family even though they knew nothing about you?

Much later, after nothing had been said to her about the immediate future, Rachel slipped on her jacket and went out. No scramble over the moors this time because she knew that Brian was safely away in Rawthwaite for the afternoon. She went through the gate, fingering Aunt Sophie's silver cross on its chain round her neck and feeling a rush of longing for her aunt.

A hand on her shoulder made her gasp. She swung round and saw Julie. Rachel smiled, sick with relief that it wasn't Brian.

"You look as if you'd seen a ghost, Rachel. Fancy a cup of tea? I'll get the kettle on. The cottage is round the corner. Will you come?"

Rachel nodded. They went out of the churchyard at the other side and rounded a bend in the track. Julie's cottage was solidly grey in an overgrown garden.

"Come on in," Julie said. "I'll not be long making tea."

Rachel glanced behind her, aware that this was Brian's home as well as Julie's. Pots of geraniums stood on the sill of the tiny, latticed window, and flowery curtains were held back by yellow bands.

"What an attractive room," she said.

Julie looked pleased as she arranged delicate china on a tray.

"My mother's family was in service at the house long since. There were other cottages around here once, farther up the gorge. You can see the ruins among the trees. I was born in the next place down, and lived there till we wed, Brian and me. He's the Woodfields' gardener now, like his dad before him. Beautiful grounds the Woodfields had then, not like it is today."

Her face clouded. Rachel gazed thoughtfully at the tea tray as Julie poured tea for them both. She hadn't yet thought of what life could be like here, especially in winter.

"But you like it here, don't you, Julie?"

Julie smiled.

"Aye."

Rachel glanced round the room. An empty silver rose bowl stood on a small table at one side of the window.

"That's lovely," she said, getting up. "May I look?"

She picked it up and carried it back to her seat. The bowl felt cold and hard, but the shape of it pleased her. She looked carefully at the intricate engravings on it. She ran her fingers over the swirls, and then turned it upside down to examine the base. She saw the usual silver mark, and something else, too, the engraved shape of a rose. She drew in her breath. It was the same rose design she had seen in Sarah Swinbank's diary!

She sat so long with her head bowed over

the silver bowl that Julie looked at her anxiously.

"Is something wrong, Rachel?"

Dazed, Rachel looked up.

"No, oh, no. It's this pretty engraving. Do you know anything about it?"

Julie took the bowl from her to examine it. She shook her head.

"It's a rose, that's all," she said, handing it back.

"I've seen something like this before."

"Aye? Pretty, isn't it? We got it when Brian's mum died."

"So you didn't buy it for yourselves? You don't know where it came from, where she bought it?"

Julie shook her head.

"His mum always liked it, and Brian does, too. He was fond of his mum, you see. But that's all I know about it. Biscuit?"

Rachel put the silver bowl down reluctantly, and then could hardly take her eyes from it. Afterwards she thought that Julie must think her crazy. Although she replied to Julie's words and drank her tea she did so in a dreamy state. Walking back through the churchyard she forgot Brian in her interest in what she had found in Brian's home. A valuable clue? Could be, if someone knew where it had come from. It was reasonable to think that some of her grandfather's work was still around in the place where he had lived and worked.

Mrs Woodfield was waiting for her on the steps of the house, and her pale face seemed carved in stone.

"Nerissa's just gone," she called.

"Gone?" Rachel cried, running to her. "But where?"

Mrs Woodfield turned to fumble with the door handle. She went slowly inside.

"I'm glad you're here, my dear. You'll stay, won't you?"

"Of course I will," Rachel cried.

"Nerissa made a list of your duties. She must have been planning to go, but she didn't tell me. Now, where have I put it? Julie will give you my breakfast tray each day to bring up, and I'll enjoy your company while I eat. Ah, here's the list. Take it, Rachel, and let me know what you think. I'll need you to accompany me on any of my rare outings, but you'll see that most afternoons will be free, evenings, too, apart from helping me to bed. And there's the post to deal with and letters to write, that sort of thing. Flowers for the house, and the menus. Will you be able to cope with all that?"

Rachel smiled.

"Just trust me."

"Have a look in the study," Mrs Woodfield said. "Sort things out for your convenience. No-one else uses the computer now, and I expect you know how. You young people seem to know about that. So clever."

"I'll be glad to see to all that for you."

"You're a good girl, Rachel, but it's a lonely life for a young girl. Nerissa's done this before, gone off without telling anyone. But she's got things planned in the way of music workshops. She travels all over the world, but this is her base. This house," Mrs Woodfield murmured as if talking to herself. "Her father wanted it for her. I kept it on for her sake. You really will stay, my dear?"

"Oh, yes."

Rachel smiled, hugging her delight to her. She would have her chance after all.

"I've got a reason for wanting to be here, a good one."

Mrs Woodfield nodded.

"I'd like to hear about it some time, Rachel. I'd better contact Simon. He'll run Julie into Harrogate tomorrow to collect my car. Nerissa always leaves it at the Metropole Hotel, and travels down to London by train. She'll have done the same this time. Perhaps you'd like to go, too? I'll make a shopping list for both of you."

She pressed both hands of the arms of her

chair to stand up.

"I'll telephone Simon now."

"Do you girls plan to drive straight back?" Simon Swinbank asked as they reached the outskirts of town next day.

"I've all the shopping to do," Julie said. "Rachel can meet me at the car in a couple of hours."

"In that case she can have coffee at the Metropole with me first," Simon said.

He smiled warmly at Rachel, the lines deepening round his mouth. Rachel smiled, too, at the sudden rush of warmth round her heart. She couldn't think of anywhere else she would rather be at this moment than here in this luxurious place with Simon. There was something about him that had attracted her from their first meeting, perhaps the faint sense of mystery that seemed to surround him. She marvelled that a man who had once been married to Nerissa should seek her own company even for the short time it would take for them to drink their coffee.

The thickly-carpeted hall felt warm and inviting. In the dining-room, spring sunshine glinted on the brass ornaments on the mantelshelf. Simon gave the order to the waitress, and leaned back in his chair.

"So you've agreed to stay on at Alderbeck, Rachel. I'm glad."

Rachel's cheeks felt warm, and she knew her eyes were shining as she gazed back at him. Had he noticed? Confused, she said the first thing that came into her head.

"D'you know where a place called Alderbeck Court is? My grandmother came from near Alderbeck, and I'm trying to find her house."

The waitress came with a coffee pot and jug of cream on a silver tray. Rachel moved slightly in her chair, anxious for her to go.

"Alderbeck Court?" Simon said. "I grew up on stories of Alderbeck Court."

Rachel's hand shook a little as she began to pour coffee for them both.

"Oh, where is it?"

"I'm sorry, Rachel. I hate to tell you. Alderbeck Court was burned down fifty years ago."

She couldn't breathe. Her breath wouldn't come. A second of sheer panic followed and then it rushed out in a gasp. She looked at him in horror.

"Burned down? But how?"

Hastily she put the pot down, spilling a little coffee on the white cloth. She watched the stain spread, hardly noticing.

"An accident, I think. No-one was hurt,

but I don't know what became of the family after that. They all dispersed. Like your grandmother, no doubt."

"She left Alderbeck before it happened."

"And she didn't tell you anything about it?"

"Nothing. You see, I never knew her. My aunt who brought me up would never tell me anything about the family. When I found my grandmother had the same surname as you, I wondered . . ."

She looked up hopefully but saw it meant nothing to Simon.

"My parents were the last of that name in these parts, and they never mentioned any other Swinbank relatives," he said.

She sighed.

"But I can go and visit the ruins of the house, can't I? Is it far?"

"If you go and look at some of the laithes on the hill above where the house used to be you'll see some of the stone. Barns, they are. They're built from stone from the house. But you'll not see anything of the ruins, Rachel, just a sheet of water stretching into the hills. The valley where Alderbeck Court stood was flooded to make a reservoir."

She picked up her cup. Her hands were steady now, though she felt them tremble.

"There were only a few houses and the people were re-housed elsewhere," he said. "There was the church, too."

She saw that his cup was empty, and she picked up the coffee pot to refill it. The skin at the corners of his mouth crinkled as he smiled his thanks.

"Millstone grit was quarried from the hillside nearby to build the dam. The dry-stone walls were built of it, too, centuries ago. If you ever go up there you'll see some of the walls disappearing into the water where the fields used to be."

She shivered.

"I hope they moved everything first, the tombstones . . ."

"Arthur Snaithe's the one to ask. He worked on a farm over that way before he came to work for us."

"So he might know something of the house?"

"A good chance. I'll ask him, or better still, you can ask him yourself. Get Mrs Woodfield to bring you over to my place, High Hob farm."

Simon wanted her to come to his home, to see it for herself! She smiled though her face felt stiff with shock from what he had told her.

"High Hob's a funny name."

"Hob was the ancient name given to spirits or hobgoblins."

The expression on his face was serious, but amusement danced in his eyes.

"Little devils. People tried to bribe them, but it did no good. They ate the plates of food left out for them, and then went on curdling the milk and tripping up the unwary. There's the tale that one old miner who said he didn't believe in them came to a bad end in Flitstone bog one dark night."

"I hope they don't live at High Hob now."

He laughed and looked at his watch.

"If they do, they're lying low."

Rachel laughed, too, trying hard to fight down her deep disappointment about Alderbeck Court. If only this precious time with Simon could last for ever, but soon the coffee was drunk, the shortbread biscuits eaten. She saw him give another quick glance at his watch, and then beckon the waitress to their table. When she had gone Simon got swiftly to his feet.

"We must be off now, Rachel. I've things to do, and so have you, I expect."

"It's so lovely here, so peaceful. I wish I could stay for ever."

She saw the sympathy in his eyes as he half-smiled at her. He knew exactly how she felt. Perhaps he felt the same way, too. She would hide that hope deep in her heart and think about it later.

CHAPTER FOUR

"So your grandmother was the young girl who ran off with Harry Brent from Rawthwaite?" Mrs Woodfield said as she lowered herself carefully into her high-backed chair at the dining table some time later. "I remember my parents talking about it years afterwards."

"You did?"

Rachel leaned forward, her heart leaping. Here was a precious link with the past! It was more than she had dared hope for when she joined Mrs Woodfield in the sitting-room when she and Julie got back from town. While Julie was busy preparing the meal Mrs Woodfield had asked her about her special reasons for wanting to be here at Alderbeck. She had poured out everything about the mystery surrounding her family that she was determined to solve as well as about the Felphams giving her a home when her aunt died.

"They sound good people," Mrs Woodfield said. "I still haven't telephoned, have I? All this business with Nerissa put it out of my head. Remind me after the meal. I'd like to have a word with your Mr Felpham."

Rachel nodded. She had written to the Felphams. As her legal guardian he might well insist she return at once. She tried hard to put the worry to the back of her mind. Now, as they helped themselves from the lamb casserole, Mrs Woodfield reminisced happily.

"I was only small myself then, of course, but I remember hearing about the fuss the elopement caused at the time. She was young and pretty, you see, and Harry was rather older."

"They must have loved each other very much," Rachel said.

They were members of her family, and that's what she needed — family. She could hardly eat for the excitement welling up inside her. Mrs Woodfield smiled as she passed the dish of carrots.

"I've old letters upstairs, Rachel, my dear. I'll go through them later on to see if I can find out any more."

"Oh, will you? Did anyone say what happened to my grandmother and Harry Brent afterwards? Did they come back here at all? What about their parents?"

Mrs Woodfield put down her knife and fork, and wiped her lips on her napkin.

"I just remember being told that it caused

a bit of a sensation at the time. And then, of course, the house burned down. That's all I know, really. It's some way from here, you see, over the hill."

Rachel nodded.

"Simon tells me he met you up on the hill the other day. I'm glad you enjoyed yourself looking around, Rachel, my dear. Your free time is your own, but I'm not happy about you wandering off on the fells by yourself."

"Oh, but . . ."

"It's not good for you to dwell on the past all the time, my dear. You need other interests as well if you're not going to be lonely here. Simon was telling me you like walking. There's that group that meets down in Rawthwaite."

"Oh, but I don't think . . ."

"They're mainly young people, more your age. I think you should join them, Rachel. There's no reason at all why you shouldn't be free all day on Saturdays. Will you go, to please me? There'll be plenty of time for detective work, too, my dear. Suppose I get Julie to run you down to Rawthwaite in the morning. Go to the Outdoor Shop and ask about the walking group. Why don't you?"

Rachel smiled.

"Right, I will."

"Good girl. I'm sure you won't regret it.

And while you've gone I'll take a look at those letters. Who knows what might turn up?"

Beds of daffodils lit up the corners of the old grey town when Rachel went down the ginnel between tall buildings next morning on the way to the Outdoor Shop. An elderly man came stooping out of the back premises as Rachel went in.

"A beginner, are you?" he asked. "Turn up here tomorrow, Saturday, lass, at eleven."

Rachel, thanking him, turned to go, but then remembered she needed boots and thick socks. He insisted she have a tin of special polish, too.

"To waterproof the boots," he said, opening the tin for her to see the yellow mess inside. "Rub your fingers over it very gently, and apply a little at a time."

Outside, the sunshine made her blink, and the brightness in the main street dazzled her. Two people walked towards her. With a flash of pain Rachel saw Simon glance at her and then at the woman at his side. She could hardly speak for the lump in her throat. She held out the white box.

"Hiking boots," she blurted out. "I've just bought them."

The woman's dainty feet were shod in neat brown shoes. Her cords were smart, and her violet jacket set off her long, straight hair as if the sun shone on that alone. Beside her Rachel felt rough and clumsy. She tried hard to smile, but she felt as if her lips were splitting the sides of her face. When they walked on she ran back to the car, glad that Julie was there with her shopping and ready to go.

At the house she rushed upstairs and went to the window of her room to look out to the hills. Simon was so much older than she was. He had been kind to her when she was lonely and worried, that was all. How could she know how it really was when no-one had told her? Did he do this with everyone, make them think they were special when all the time there was someone else?

A spasm of agony shot through her like a dagger. Had she been stupid not to have known that kindness was all it was, on Simon's side at least? But there wasn't the slightest hint in the warmth of his eyes, his smile that seemed specially for her, until she had seen him look at the woman walking beside him. But why shouldn't he have someone else? He was an attractive man. The pain of it was unbearable.

She took the lid off the white box, and lifted out her new boots. Opening the lid of the tin of yellow ointment, she rubbed her fingers across the smooth surface, liking the waxy smell. After a while she felt it melt slightly, and began to work it into the leather. Backwards and forwards went her fingers until all the greasy ointment was absorbed. She carried the boots back to the window, and looked at them as if she had never seen boots before. Then she placed them side by side on the carpet where she could see them each time she came into the room.

Several people stood waiting at the far end of the ginnel as Rachel walked along it at eleven o'clock next morning. Their breath on the chilly air hung about them like shiny mist, and heavy boots scraped the cobbles underfoot. She heard footsteps behind her, and turned to see a young man only a little older than herself. He smiled at her with warmth in his eyes.

"You'll be the girl Ken was telling me about. I'm David."

Rachel smiled uncertainly.

"Hi, David."

She was drawn into the group immediately and asked how much walking she had done, while David, his fair curly hair showing beneath his green woolly hat, discussed the route for the day. As he talked he removed his hat and stuffed it in the pocket of his brown cords.

"Not a long walk today," he told Rachel as they climbed a stile and began to walk up a hillocky field.

She was relieved, not wanting to hold everyone back.

"How far are we going?"

He laughed. The skin on his face was smooth, and his hair was so curly it looked as if he had crinkled it for the occasion.

"I'm not saying."

It was great being treated like one of the others. They reached another stile in a stone wall, higher this time, and waited their turn to climb it. After passing through a thin wood they came out on to rough ground again, still climbing. Ahead of them Rachel saw the dark moors rising to a clear sky. In David's encouraging presence she began to lose her worry that she might not be able to keep up with the others as mile followed mile. One or two of them were behind them now.

They reached the brow of a hill, and Rachel stood still in surprise. Ahead stretched the calm surface of a long stretch of water. She saw the dam built at one end, and the reflections of the bare hills on the other side. Could it be? She quickly found David and asked him.

"Garth Scar Reservoir," he told her.

Garth Scar, the reservoir that covered Alderbeck Court! As they made their way down to it she slipped once or twice because her eyes were on the clear water instead of on the rough ground beneath her feet. The young Sarah Swinbank would have seen those same heathery hills on the other side. The thought gave her such a jolt, she stopped.

"What's wrong?" David asked.

"Nothing, oh, nothing."

He grinned at her. As they moved on down together she saw an old stone building halfway up the hill on the other side of the reservoir. Could it be the barn Simon told her about that had been repaired with some of the stone from the house? She felt breathless suddenly.

Reaching the water's edge, they all spread out and seated themselves on rocks to eat their lunch. Rachel looked across at the barn on the hill where the dark mass of heather met the top of one of the narrow stone-walled fields. She had the strangest feeling. For a moment she felt like the young Sarah. She knew how she must have felt all those long years ago, the wrench at leaving her home and family. She knew, also, the overpowering love she had for her

59

young husband.

"Aren't you going to eat?" David asked.

She was startled. For a moment David seemed unreal. Only the stone barn had significance for her because of its connection with Alderbeck Court. She knew she would come here again, often.

"That building up there," she said, pointing to it. "What is it?"

David took a huge bite from his sandwich, and chewed for a moment in silence.

"Up there on the side of the hill?" he asked when he had swallowed. "There are lots of those. Laithes, barns, I mean."

"I've heard of laithes," she said, thinking of her conversation with Simon.

"Interested in old buildings?" David went on.

"Yes, I mean not really. Only that one up there."

"A good specimen. Useful to the farmer, of course. Probably been there for years."

"At least fifty," she said dreamily.

Gradually she became aware of the others speaking to each other, and she was back with them again. She undid her bag, placed her Thermos flask on the ground nearby and began to eat the pork pie and tomatoes Julie had packed for her. David flipped open a can of juice and began to drink. Rachel thought of Mrs Woodfield wanting her to make friends. Could it be this easy?

One of the younger boys sprang up and started to leap from boulder to boulder. He stood poised, silhouetted against the shining water, a dark human shape in the vast expanse of nothingness. Rachel watched him. She could hardly believe she was here. Even the air seemed different.

It wasn't until they were back in Rawthwaite in the carpark that she realised how exhausted she felt. She leaned on the wall with her head bent. David walked across to her.

"OK, Rachel? Are you being met?"

She indicated the car on the other side of him.

"Julie's around somewhere. She won't be long. I said I'd meet her here."

She bent to unlace her boots, slipped her feet out of them and wriggled her toes.

"That's better. I'll have to give them more practice."

David smiled, and her eyes looked bright.

"Tomorrow? I could show you Shutt Hob Gorge. We'd come out on the top farther over from today. It's hidden among some trees you passed on your way down to Rawthwaite. It's worth seeing. Want to come?"

Rachel smiled. Why not? She had to find

something else to stop her thinking about Simon all the time.

"All right. It'll have to be the afternoon."

"We'll meet where the track joins the road."

"Wait a minute," she called after him as he strode off. "What time?"

He spun round.

"Good thinking. Two o'clock?"

This time Rachel was better equipped. Her boots were washed and greased, a woolly hat was on her head and Julie's old green cagoule was in the borrowed rucksack on her back. She also knew that another way into Shutt Hob Gorge was along the track past Julie's cottage on the other side of the churchyard.

There was no sign of David as Rachel walked down the road from Alderbeck House to the belt of trees where the track met the road. Then there was the sound of a car engine, and he was there in his brown cords and blue cagoule with his bushy fair hair standing up more than ever. He looked cheerful as he leaped out of the white car he had parked by the wall. He patted it proudly.

"Like her?" he said. "She's Mum's really, but I get to drive on my own sometimes."

"Lucky you," Rachel said, smiling, too.

He took only moments to change into his hiking boots and sling a small rucksack on his back. At first the going was easy as they set off. They walked through the trees, scuffling through damp brown leaves that muffled their footsteps, until they reached another path that joined their own. They walked on and soon the path narrowed between high limestone cliffs overhung with bare trees. It was easy to believe in Simon's sprites and hobgoblins in this eerie place. Water dripped down the grey rocks.

"Like it?" David said cheerfully. "Spooky, isn't it? Ghosts and boggarts here abound. That's a quotation from one of our local poets. My interest's history, not literature, but he's got something there. Wait till you see the waterfalls farther up."

"You're still at school?" Rachel asked.

David nodded.

" 'A'-levels, then university, I hope."

The gorge was narrower now. The sound of dripping water intensified, and Rachel saw the glint of shining cascades through the bare branches of the trees as they walked towards it.

"Fantastic, isn't it?" David shouted above the noise of the crashing water echoing among the cliffs.

The spray caressed Rachel's face as she

stared in awe.

"Watch this," David cried as he ran towards the waterfall.

He walked carefully on the narrow path against the cliff and then disappeared behind the water to come out moments later on the other side.

"Come on, Rachel. It's fun."

She went nearer, but not too near. He came back towards her, vanished for a moment and then there was a flash of blue and he was beside her again.

"You won't get wet behind the waterfall. The water shoots out at an angle from the top of the cliff."

Rachel pressed herself against the cliff, past rocks covered in green moss, edging herself carefully along until she stood at David's side looking upwards at the force of spray shooting down past them. But here, behind the fall of water, she felt less spray on her face than when she stood in front of it.

"I enjoyed that," she said when they came out again and moved on along the path which now climbed steeply until it reached bare moorland.

The colder air whipped colour into her cheeks. She pulled her woolly hat over her ears and zipped her cagoule up to her neck.

They stopped to lean against a drystone wall and looked at the view before them. As David began to talk about Alderdale and the thriving craft centre it had once been, Rachel's interest quickened.

"Rawthwaite Museum has got an exhibition on of some of the small workshops that used to be in the town," he said. "They've got all the old tools and everything."

Rachel felt colour flow into her cheeks. Here was a lead she wasn't expecting!

"My grandfather was a craftsman in Rawthwaite," she said. "D'you think . . ."

"He was? Interesting. What sort of craftsman?" David interrupted.

"A silver engraver. I don't know much about him. I'm trying to find out. That's why I took the job at Alderbeck House looking after Mrs Woodfield. I wanted to be here on the spot you see, not in London."

"Could be worth a visit to the museum to see if there's anything of his there. What was his name?"

"Harry Brent. Have you heard of him?"

He wrinkled his nose, thinking hard.

"Tell me some more about him."

Rachel, breathless with excitement, told David all she knew as they retraced their steps. It was little enough, really, but David's interest and sympathy invited confidences. She liked the way he altered his stride to match hers. When he suggested another meeting, she agreed at once.

CHAPTER FIVE

To Rachel's dismay a taxi drew up outside the front door of Alderbeck House as she walked up the drive. Nerissa, in bright red, stepped out daintily. At once Brian was there, too, greeting her as if they hadn't seen each other for months. Brian welcoming Nerissa home, standing close? Incredible. As Rachel watched, the taxi driver slung a couple of smart suitcases out of the back and carried them to the front door.

Rachel turned and ran, her mind churning. In the kitchen Julie was banging a milk jug down on the tray so hard that white drops flew everywhere. With a sigh she took everything off the tray, threw the cloth in the sink and then took another from a drawer. As she spun round on her high heels Rachel saw that her face was flushed.

"She's back."

"Nerissa? I saw them . . . er . . . her."

"Worrying her mum and all, and Mrs Woodfield with her bad heart."

"Has Nerissa come back for good?" Rachel asked.

"Who knows?"

Rachel murmured something, and then escaped. It was plain that Nerissa's arrival didn't please Julie. And what would it mean for herself if Nerissa decided to come back for good after all? It didn't bear thinking about.

Later, when the greetings were over and Nerissa was upstairs in her room, Mrs Woodfield joined the girls in the kitchen. Rachel looked anxiously at her employer's strained face. Julie drew out a chair for her to sit down.

"I think I'll go up soon myself, Rachel," Mrs Woodfield said. "Did Nerissa tell you she'd like a tray upstairs, Julie?"

"Aye," Julie said, looking grim. "I'll bring one up for you, too."

Rachel sprang up to help her employer up to her room.

"You're a good girl, Rachel," Mrs Woodfield murmured as she seated herself on her bed. "How did the walk go today?"

Rachel told her quickly, unable to keep the excitement out of her voice when she came to the news that David had told her about the workshops in the museum and her hope that her grandfather's might be among them. She was pleased to see that by the time Mrs Woodfield was in bed she looked a little less strained.

"That one upstairs!" Julie spat out when Rachel opened the kitchen door next morning.

Julie thumped a cup and saucer down on a tray.

"I've been here hours with all the cleaning to do. Now Nerissa wants her breakfast taking up."

"I'll take it," Rachel said.

She glanced at the tray. From the pot came whiffs of fresh coffee.

"Want some?" Julie asked, grabbing the pot and splashing some into a mug for Rachel.

She refilled the pot from the kettle. Rachel giggled.

"Nerissa always get me like this," Julie snapped as she opened the door for Rachel. "She'll worry her mum sick. It's not good for Mrs Woodfield with her bad heart and all."

There was no sound from Nerissa's bedroom when Rachel knocked on the door and went in. She placed the tray on the bedside table and looked nervously at the hump in the bed. The dark curtains cut out the morning sun that brightened the kitchen, but the room was stifling. She

68

switched on the table lamp, and turned to leave.

"Wait!"

Nerissa sat up, and pushed her hair away from her face.

"Have you got Mother up yet?"

"Her back was bad yesterday, and I thought . . ."

"You're not paid to think."

Rachel shrugged. For a moment she felt like making a sharp retort but then thought better of it.

"I'll see if she needs me yet."

Mrs Woodfield was struggling to sit up. She smiled at Rachel as she went in and drew open the curtains. Outside a few clouds floated in a sky so blue it looked radiant.

"It's a lovely day," Rachel told her.

"We need to make plans, my dear. I thought a visit to the museum this morning. You'd like that, wouldn't you?"

Rachel's heart leaped.

"If you feel up to it."

"Of course I do. I'm so much better today. How fortunate that the young man knew about the craft workshops."

She frowned.

"I'm just sorry there was no mention of anything that would interest you in those old letters of mine. I went through them with a fine tooth comb but nothing at all about Alderbeck Court. Never mind, we'll be on the look-out for clues today."

Rachel could hardly contain her excitement as they descended to the musty atmosphere of the museum basement where the trappings of the trades that used to flourish in the area were displayed. It felt like going down into another, magical world where wonderful things happened that sparked light from the dingy walls to turn them into gold. She blinked, surprised that this didn't happen as they passed along the line of workshops. Each was in an arched alcove.

Rachel had eyes for only one, and she found it in seconds. A board above the doorway read: H. BRENT, ENGRAVER. A surge of pure joy shot through her.

"Look!" she breathed.

This was it. This little workshop was the place where her grandfather spent hours of his life. Entranced, she gazed at the framed certificates on the walls and at the engraver's tools laid out on the wooden workbench. At her side Mrs Woodfield looked, too, holding the wall for support.

"Oh, Rachel, what a thrill. The tools look as if they've only just been used, that he put them there himself only a minute ago."

Rachel stared hard at the workbench as if that could tell her all she wanted to know. The wooden handles of the tools were old and worn as if they had been used for many years. They looked quite ordinary, except that she knew her grandfather had held them in his sensitive hands as he made beautiful patterns with them in silver.

What work had Harry Brent done after he and Sarah Swinbank ran away? Surely something quite different or his tools and workbench wouldn't be here in the museum now, or had he bought a new set when he and Sarah started their new life together?

"I wonder what sort of man he was," Mrs Woodfield murmured.

Rachel wondered that, too. She thought of Harry engrossed in his intricate work, his head bent over this same bench. He would be thinking of Sarah and their secret plans to escape to another place far away where they would live happily ever after.

"I wonder where his workshop actually was," she said. "Somewhere in Rawthwaite, I suppose."

"The curator will know," Mrs Woodfield said. "We'll ask him. I wonder who presented the tools to the museum."

Rachel gazed at them for a few moments longer and then turned her attention to the framed certificates on the wall. It was good to know that other people beside herself could see that her grandfather had been skilled in his job. The pride she felt made her feel taller, older. She was a better person because of this knowledge she had found here today.

Mrs Woodfield gave a little sigh.

"Have you seen enough for the moment, Rachel? Shall we find the curator?"

Rachel glanced back once as they moved towards the staircase. The basement no longer seemed dank and dreary. Because of what she had found there the lights seemed brighter, and the air warm. Halfway up the stairs Mrs Woodfield stopped suddenly, and clutched her heart. Rachel sprang round, alarmed.

"I'm all right," Mrs Woodfield gasped. "No need for fuss."

She held on to the rail and pulled herself up the remaining steps and then stood, white-faced and breathless. The curator hurried to them with his pen in one hand.

"Stay there, madam. I'll get a chair."

Mrs Woodfield sank down gratefully.

"We came to see the silver engraver's workshop. Harry Brent."

"Oh, please, don't talk," Rachel begged.

She looked at the curator.

"Water?"

He went to get some, and returned with a glass in his hand. He hovered round them for a moment or two until the telephone rang.

"I'll get a doctor," Rachel said.

But Mrs Woodfield handed her the empty glass and struggled to her feet.

"Now we're here we'll find out what we can. The curator . . ."

She gave a little gasp.

"I'll come back another time. The doctor . . ."

"Will be out of his rounds, my dear. I'm so sorry to be like this."

"It doesn't matter," Rachel cried. "Please sit down and rest."

But Mrs Woodfield set off at once, and Rachel had to follow. Arriving at the car, she was glad to see more colour now in the older woman's cheeks, but she insisted that Mrs Woodfield rest for a few minutes on the low stone wall that separated the car-park from the river. They talked gently for a while and then Mrs Woodfield pressed both hands on the wall at her side and levered herself up. She gave a cry of triumph.

"Rachel! Now I know what it is. My bad back, remember? I always do this now to stand up, and the muscles across my chest take the strain. That's what it is all the time, not my heart at all, just muscle strain."

Rachel looked at her doubtfully.

"I think you should make sure."

"Don't fuss, dear. What a relief! Wait till I tell Nerissa, and Julie."

She got in the car with Rachel beside her, still talking.

When they returned, David Swinbank's white car was parked in the drive of Alderbeck House. Rachel leaped out of Mrs Woodfield's car as soon as it stopped.

"David, what are you doing here?"

He smiled, his fair hair looking bushier than ever.

"I've got something for you, Rachel. I couldn't wait to show you."

Mrs Woodfield, joining them, smiled.

"Take him inside, my dear, and get Julie to make some coffee. You'll have time for that, won't you? You can tell Julie I'm upstairs. Now, Rachel, dear, I'm all right. You can stop worrying and look after the young man."

They went into the kitchen. Julie, busy preparing vegetables at the sink, turned round beaming, and immediately filled the kettle and plugged it in.

"I'll not take long," she said to David. "You'll be one of the walking group. Are you taking part in the Cravon Walk this year? Brian always does."

David grinned.

"You bet. I wouldn't miss it for anything."

"Mrs Woodfield's not well, Julie," Rachel said. "I think I ought to . . ."

"I'll check on her in a minute," Julie said.

As soon as they were alone, David got a small packet out of his pocket.

"It's for you, Rachel. Another clue."

She unwrapped it with trembling fingers, and found a tiny, engraved coin.

"What is it? Where did you get it?"

"It's an old silver threepenny piece, engraved on both sides. I was down in Rawthwaite, and I saw it in the window of that little junk shop at the top of the street."

"Someone's engraved a picture of Shutt Hob Gorge on it!"

She held the tiny thing in her hand. Queen Victoria's head took up most of the space on one side, but squashed between her and the Roman lettering were the words: **From Harry to Rose 1910.**

"My grandfather's work? Yes, of course it is," she said.

She looked up in excitement.

"We've been to the museum, David, to see his workshop. It's there like you said, and his tools and everything. But, David,

75

who is Rose?"

Their heads were close together as they examined the wording on the coin, but at the opening of the door they sprang apart. Simon stood on the threshold. He looked at them in surprise, a frown creasing his forehead.

"I'm interrupting."

Rachel felt herself flush as he withdrew. David, intent on the coin, appeared not to notice. Still feeling uncomfortable, Rachel turned back to him.

"So who was Rose? My grandmother's name was Sarah."

David whistled.

"Tricky that. Could it have been the name he called his wife, your grandmother — a sort of nickname?"

"Could be," Rachel said doubtfully, thinking of the rose design at the end of the diary.

An engraved rose was on his brass plate in the museum, also. It would have meant so much, once, and now they were both dead, Harry and Sarah.

"It's so sad. So long ago, and I only know about them because of the diary."

"Not to worry," he said cheerfully when he finished his coffee. "We'll find out more, somehow. I'll have to go. See you next

76

Saturday? We've another walk planned."

"I'll be there," she said. "And thanks for the silver coin, David."

As soon as he had gone Rachel went to look for Julie but hesitated in the hall as she saw Simon. He smiled as he came forward.

"I'm sorry about that, lass."

"It's all right. It's nothing."

She was relieved that he had waited so she could tell him about Mrs Woodfield's sudden turn in the museum. He frowned.

"So you won't believe this has a simple explanation, Rachel?"

"I thought someone should know what happened. She says it's muscle strain."

"Could be. Where is she now, upstairs?"

"I'll tell her you're here, shall I?"

"Don't bother. She won't mind if I go up to her. It's just some papers to sign, that's all. And I'll insist she sees the doctor for a check up."

He smiled at her briefly, and was gone.

Rachel went to look for Julie, and found her in the sitting-room with a duster in her hand.

"I'll do that," she offered.

"If you want a job you can take a list he wanted to Brian for me. It's in the kitchen. He'll be out seeing to the rosebeds."

The list was on the windowsill. With it in

her hand Rachel went out again into the mild spring air, looking for Brian. He seemed to have finished what he was doing and was packing some small tools in a canvas bag. She held out the forgotten list.

"Is this what you wanted? Julie said to bring it."

He grinned, and took it from her.

"And not the only thing I'm wanting either, lass."

She felt his warm breath as he took a step nearer. For a horrified moment she thought he would grab her. She recoiled, and then turned and ran. Safe indoors, she stopped in the hall to regain her breath, pushing all thoughts of Brian to the back of her mind. When her breathing subsided and she was calm again she got out the silver coin. Carefully she unwrapped the tissue in which she had put it for safekeeping.

Sunlight glittered on the lettering. Incredible that her grandfather's hands had once touched this as he worked this delicate engraving. She had a sudden picture of him bending over his workbench in concentration.

A sound on the staircase made her look up. Simon was there with the lines round his eyes deepening as he smiled at her. Her heart leaped as it always did when she saw him.

"What's that you've got there, Rachel? May I look?"

With trembling fingers she showed it to him.

"So another of these has come to light?"

He sounded amused.

"A naughty boy, our Harry, defacing coins of the realm. Illegal, of course. He'd have known that and kept them within the family when he did them. Showing off his skills, I suppose. This was a silver threepenny bit. Did you know that?"

She shook her head.

"You know about Harry Brent? But how?"

"He did quite a lot of them. York Minster was a favourite subject, and the Lord's Prayer. A difficult thing to do, that. Nothing wrong with them now, of course, because these things went out of circulation before the Second World War. Harry was a prolific lad. Brian's not a bit like him."

"Brian?"

"Aye, Brian. Harry's great-grandson, is Brian. Look!"

He held the coin out to her.

"From Harry to Rose — Brian's great grandparents."

She stared at him, speechless.

"Zachary, Brian's grandad, wasn't interested in carrying on the craft. A pity."

He looked at her in sudden concern.

"Why, Rachel, what's wrong?"

She tried to speak but couldn't for the tightness in her throat. It wasn't true. It couldn't be! Rose and Harry, not Sarah and Harry. If Harry Brent was married to Rose, what about Sarah? It wasn't like she imagined, the young couple running off together to start a family. That wasn't the way of it at all. She swallowed hard.

"I'm all right."

"I'll not keep you then. Mrs Woodfield sounded fine, but I'll be in touch. Nerissa not here today?"

Rachel shook her head. She didn't care whether she was or not. First there was the effort of coping with her feelings each time she saw Simon, and now this. It was almost too much to bear.

He nodded, and she left him, going blindly upstairs to her room. She sank down on her bed, and tried to stop her hands trembling. The coin was back in her pocket. She got it out and thrust it into the bottom of her top drawer. She didn't want to look at it again, ever. Her feeling of deep loss numbed her.

She was a stranger here among strangers. She didn't belong. Simon's thoughts were all with that woman he was with in Raw-thwaite as Harry's were with Rose when he engraved her name with his. Simon's casual words of information about that meant that something of importance had been taken from her. She no longer belonged anywhere. She was imprisoned in a well of deep noth-ingness.

CHAPTER SIX

"I shouldn't have given you the silver coin, should I?" David said. "You see I thought Rose was Harry's special name for your grandmother."

Rachel shivered but said nothing. In the misty distance the hills looked pale. Nearer at hand the grass was beginning to show deep green. She moved her position slightly against the drystone wall.

"Do you think Harry and Sarah got mar-ried afterwards?"

"Does it matter? You can believe anything you want, and it doesn't hurt anybody."

"Because they're dead? But it hurts me if I don't know."

Her hair fell forward as she bent her head.

"Rose and Harry had a son, Zachary. Si-mon said he was a bad lot. D'you think it spread down to Zachary's daughter, and then to Brian?"

David looked at her closely.

"Brian been trying it on?"

"Not really."

"He'd better not."

"I didn't mean that. He's rotten to Julie, that's what I meant. I think he hits her sometimes. It's a shock, knowing Brian and I are related."

"Does he know that?"

She shuddered.

"No way. I mean . . . I hope not. He's horrible. I wanted to find out things about the past, but now I wish I hadn't."

David's bushy hair shone fair in the sunshine, and his eyes were bright.

"We have to know about the past to make sense of the present."

Rachel said nothing. The present made no sense, either. When Mrs Woodfield had phoned Mr Felpham yesterday evening he had asked to speak to her. For a moment, hearing his deep, familiar voice, tears had sprung to her eyes. He was a link with Aunt Sophie who had relied on him for advice. He had sounded hurt at first, and she couldn't blame him. It was hard to explain why she had run off to take up a job in the North of England but in the end he had seemed to understand. Then he had blamed himself for giving her the diary in the first place when she was still so vulnerable.

"What's wrong, Rachel?" David said. "You're not going to give up, are you?"

She shrugged and then shivered. Give up what — this feeling that she didn't belong anywhere? In any case, Mrs Woodfield's back was so much better, and she fully expected the doctor to endorse her belief that her heart was no problem. She had Julie, and Nerissa was home every now and again. Mrs Woodfield didn't need anyone else now so her own days here were numbered. There'd be no time to unearth anything else even if she wanted to, and she didn't.

"Come on, let's go. You still want to visit Garth Scar?" David said suddenly.

She hesitated, and then nodded. David had gone to a lot of trouble to arrange for the two of them to deviate from the planned route today and to join the rest of the group at a certain point later. He had done it in such a way through Ken that no-one made any funny remarks. If she changed her mind now the explanations could be embarrassing.

She followed him to the summit. The path was gone, but David knew where to go.

"It's so wild up here," she said on the way

83

up. "And it all looks the same with all this heather. I'm glad you're here, too, David. I'd have got lost."

He flushed, looking pleased.

"It's OK today, but wait till the cloud comes down. That's the time to get worried."

She could believe it. Today she could see the top of the land against the sky. How would she feel if it was all blotted out and she was the only person for miles around? A faint smell of burning wafted across the hillside as they neared the edge of the brow and looked down on the sheet of calm water. Rachel stopped suddenly.

"What's going on?"

David waved his hand.

"Over there, look!"

To their right two men were climbing on a tractor which set off with a roar across the blackened ground to a track at the bottom.

"Firing the heather," David said. "No wonder we smelled burning."

"But why?"

"Keeps the heather low-growing. You're not worried? It grows again."

She gave a shaky smile, reminded suddenly of the burning of Alderbeck Court. The same bitter smell would have filled the air then, but more than this, much more.

The whole valley would have been thick with it, and the crackling flames would have leaped in the air.

David caught hold of her hand briefly and gave it a comforting squeeze.

"Don't worry about it, Rachel. Burning off the heather happens all the time, in one place or the other. D'you want to go over to see the barn?"

She nodded. The stone barn stood beneath the belt of blackened heather, and by the time they reached it their jeans were criss-crossed in wavy black lines.

"It's a drystone barn," David said. "No cement or putty. Clever, don't you think?"

Rachel gazed at it. The stones used in the building of the barn were rectangular and even. To think they were taken from the ruins of Sarah Swinbank's house! Some were slightly blackened. She ran her hand over the rough wall and felt a thrill of discovery shoot up her arm. The stone seemed alive, but it couldn't be. She moved her hand away and then put it back again. The warmth was still there, as if the stone had taken on a life of its own. She gasped.

"What is it?"

"Feel it, David."

He put his hand where hers had been.

"What does it feel like to you?"

"Warm, from the sun."

"More than that."

Her voice quivered.

"Try again."

"The sun's been on it for hours. Of course it's warm. Come away, Rachel."

She felt shaky, and very odd. He moved towards her, a soft look in his eyes she found disturbing. She sprang away from him, suddenly breathless.

"I don't believe it."

She clenched and unclenched her hands, not knowing what she believed or who she was. And she couldn't account for the frightening guilt that filled her when she rested her hand on the stone barn. Suddenly she ran down the hillside to stand at the water's edge. Breathing deeply, she stared across the glassy water to where she thought the house should be. David followed.

"Rachel," he said gently, "you wanted to come, but we don't have to come again."

She let out a long breath, and her commonsense rose to the surface. No, she needn't come again. There wouldn't be time anyway. David wasn't to blame.

"I'm scared of what Arthur Snaithe's going to tell me. He works at High Hob. It's been arranged for me to go and see him."

"That's great!"

"But I don't want to any more."

She quivered, knowing she was caught up in all of this now whether she liked it or not.

"I'm glad we came today to see the place again, but I don't want to know any more about the people."

And she didn't want to see Simon at home now, either. The pain was too great. David looked surprised.

"But you can't separate place and people. What can this chap say anyway to scare you? Only that the dale was flooded half a century ago. He'd only have been a young lad then."

"I keep forgetting it all happened fifty years ago. It all seems like yesterday."

"Get it in perspective, Rachel. Fifty years is a long time. Half a century."

But she couldn't get it in perspective. She couldn't get her feeling about Simon into perspective either. She thought of the first time she had seen the reservoirs on the way from the station with Simon. Different reservoirs, but all supplying much-needed water to the cities. Other homes, besides Alderbeck Court, were lost beneath the water. The knowledge was as horrifying to her now as it had been then. She couldn't get it out of her mind.

Later, as they joined the others at a bridge over the river to eat their lunch, Rachel picked up a pebble and held it in her hand so that warmth seemed to spread into it. The stone was prettily marked with darker grey threads on the pale background. She gazed at it, suddenly filled with wonder. The stone had lain here for years and years. Her fingers moved gently over the surface, and brought a sense of peace. It was weak and stupid to be afraid of what Arthur Snaithe could tell her.

It was all in the past anyway, as David said. And why should Brian know anything about them being distantly related? If he'd known already he'd have come out with it for sure. So he had no idea, and she wasn't about to tell him.

"Arthur's in the barn," Simon said. "You'll want to talk to him."

Rachel's mouth felt dry. Simon looked so alive and vital standing there with the sunlight on his hair and an expression of deep understanding in his eyes. She longed to take a step towards him, to be enfolded in his strong arms and to press her flushed face against his chest. Fly stood at his side, tongue lolling, as if he wouldn't be surprised by anything.

She swung her loose hair away from her face, and blinked in the bright sunlight. High Hob farm was high on the fells, sheltered from the north by a belt of ash trees not yet in leaf. They had heard the bleating of lambs filling the clear air as Mrs Woodfield drove her car through the open gateway.

"I thought the lambs would be inside," she said for something to say as she walked beside Simon across the cobbled yard.

"Soon they'll be up on the fells for the summer," he said. "We've done well this year. Cross breeding has paid off. Take as long as you like, Rachel."

He stood aside for Rachel to go into the barn on her own and at once she felt abandoned. There was something so trustworthy and loving about Simon that hurt her to think about. She took a deep breath and concentrated on the reason for her being here. And yet it wasn't, not any more. She wanted to be with Simon with an intensity that shook her.

As her eyes became used to the gloomy interior of the barn she was conscious of space that dwarfed the bales of hay and the tarpaulins that lay on the ground. A faint, musty smell hung in the air. She saw the old man bending over something in the corner. He was almost invisible in his rough brown clothes until he came forward to be introduced. Then she saw a pair of twinkling eyes set deep in his ruddy face. He put down his metal pail with a clatter.

"Aye," he said. "It's a grand day."

Rachel agreed, then hesitated. He seemed not to know why she was here, and she hardly knew how to begin. Arthur scratched his grey head.

"Happen you've seen the lambs?"

Rachel said she had.

"Aye, Mrs Woodfield likes to come each year. She's a grand lady."

"She's looking at them now."

"We've a fine lot this year. Aye, a fine lot. Simon likes to show people, but now he's got no-one since his wife left. Aye, I'd like to see him suited."

"You used to work near my grandmother's home, Alderbeck Court, didn't you?"

She thought he wouldn't admit it. He scratched his head again and looked at the straw at his feet.

"Aye, lass," he said slowly.

He took a pipe from his pocket, looked at it and put it back again. Rachel sat down on a bale of straw and tried to look as if she wasn't desperately interested.

"Aye," he said again. "Your grandmother."

"It was a long time ago."

"A grand valley, where the big house was. There were a mill, too, closed long since. Folk moved out. The cottages were left empty. Aye, they were."

"And the people in the house? Did you know them?"

"Aye, I did that. My dad said there was nowt anyone could do for the poor lady when her daughter fled with a man old enough to be her dad. She never lived to see the house burned down, and when they came to move her she weren't there."

"Move her?"

"Aye, move her grave with the rest."

Rachel had thought about the headstones being moved from the churchyard, but not the graves themselves. She could see now that they couldn't be left beneath the waters of the reservoir. She looked at him in horror.

"You mean her coffin wasn't there to be moved with the others?"

A sweet, pungent smell from the straw beneath his feet reached her.

"Aye, tragic," he said. "I were only a little lad, but I remember the men coming with their spades and shovels. They buried the coffins at Beckthorpe, but they never found the mother's coffin. And then the dale were flooded. I were at the last service in church before that happened. When the water's low in the reservoir you can see the tower sticking up in the air."

Rachel, imagining the shimmering ripple of the church tower near the surface as the water level dropped, shuddered. The church again, sticking up through the innocent sheet of water. Did Sarah's mother know about Harry Brent being married when Sarah ran off with him? Of course she did. Harry was a local man, and Rose would be left behind with her son, Zachary, who grew up to become Brian's grandfather.

She thanked Arthur and left. All of a sudden a feeling of dizziness came over her and she put out a hand on the door jamb to steady herself. Then moving slowly as if in a dream she came out into the sunshine of the yard. The cobbles seemed to dissolve in front of her and the next moment Simon was there.

For a long wonderful moment he held her in his arms, supporting her. Sighing, she rested her head against him and he bent and kissed her gently. She had never before felt this deep certainty that his presence gave her but to him it was nothing. She sighed, not wanting to move away from his side, ever. But she knew she must though it was agony to feel him withdraw.

He looked at her anxiously as she stood in the sunlit yard, her hands clenched at her side.

"Rest for a while," he said, his voice gruff. "You've had a shock, Rachel. We won't go indoors until you feel better."

He led her towards the field gate at the side of the yard. They leaned there side by side, watching the lambs wobbling about near their mothers in the field. Suddenly tears filled her eyes. She knew how it felt to love someone it didn't seem possible could love you. The anguish of being near Simon and yet feeling the pain of that was unbearable. It took all her concentration to remember the woman in Rawthwaite. Simon was kind. He would never hurt anyone intentionally, neither must she.

Harry had been years older than Sarah Swinbank. Simon was years older that herself. But she wasn't going to hurt anybody so why did she feel guilty as if it was all her fault?

Garth Scar reservoir filled Rachel's dreams that night as well as Simon. The two seemed connected in a way that made her tremble. Simon's slow smile had illuminated his face as he helped her towards the support of the gate and there had been an expression in his eyes she hadn't seen before.

She tried to put it all out of her mind next morning as she helped Mrs Woodfield pick some daffodils for the house, but she couldn't help thinking of Simon's interest in what she had learned from Arthur Snaithe. His smile had faded at once when she told him what Arthur Snaithe had said about the missing coffin.

"Don't think about it," he had advised.

But in her dream it was mixed up with her feelings for Simon which she must keep buried, dead hopes that she should never have entertained from the beginning. Yet Arthur had said he would like to see Simon suited, that he had no-one since Nerissa left. But was that true? No-one had mentioned the woman she had seen him with. Perhaps she was just a friend he had bumped into in Rawthwaite and meant nothing more to him than that. But she dared not hope.

Now, in the sunny garden with the mist hanging round the tops of the hills, Rachel sighed.

"You're looking sad, my dear," Mrs Woodfield said.

She straightened, rubbed her back and looked at Rachel in concern.

"I'm not sure all this delving into the past

is good for you. I thought finding your grandfather's workshop in the museum was a breakthrough. Don't you want to go there again, and question the curator, or the library? They might be able to help you there, Rachel. Had you thought of that? You're not a prisoner here, you know. Why not get that nice young lad to go with you?"

"David?"

"Yes, David. It's grand that you've made friends. One day you'll look back on this period of your life and see that things have a way of working out for the best. They have for me, through you, my dear."

"Me?"

Her employer smiled.

"Had I not accompanied you to the museum I might never have realised that what I imagined were heart pains were nothing more than strained muscles. The doctor agrees with me. I have a slight heart murmur, but nothing much, and nothing like as bad as I thought. It was sitting on that wall afterwards that made me realise. And now look at me, as fit as a fiddle."

Not quite, Rachel thought. Mrs Woodfield still had that pallor about her cheeks. She was a brave lady, able to cope with things without complaining. She was glad for her sake that she was no longer worried about her heart even though it meant that she, herself, wasn't really needed now. Her usefulness was over, and soon Mrs Woodfield would realise it for herself.

"Julie will run you down to Rawthwaite this afternoon. It's her shopping day so there'll be plenty of time."

Mrs Woodfield looked so anxious that Rachel smiled.

"I'll phone and see if David's free," she said.

The museum, or the library — no! But David wanted to know what Arthur Snaithe had to say and she owed him that at least.

What did it matter what Sarah and Harry had done? The present mattered but that was all. Her aunt had been wiser than she knew.

Later, in the carpark in Rawthwaite, David looked so cheerful that Rachel's spirits began to lift.

"So where's it to be then, Rachel? The museum, or would you rather walk by the River Alder instead, and talk?"

"The river, please."

Surprisingly, he began to talk about the Craven Walk and brushed aside her tentative remarks about Garth Scar as if it had no importance for either of them.

"You're going to help out at the check

point at Alderbeck House tomorrow, aren't you, Rachel? Lucky it's on the route. Brian planned it that way."

"Brian?"

"Brian Hepinstall, one of the organisers. His wife, Julie, does the food for the party tomorrow night. She said you'd help."

"I didn't know Brian was involved."

"Does it make any difference?"

She hesitated, then shook her head. They came at last to where the path left the river and wound up to the top of a low hill.

"Race you to the top," David said suddenly.

They got there together, and sank to the ground, laughing. For a moment there was silence as they gazed back to the grey houses of the town and the hills beyond. He picked a piece of grass, and began to chew it. He looked serious.

"I don't want Garth Scar to frighten you," he said, "or the warmth from that barn on the hill."

"There's something else now," she said quickly. "I found it out yesterday, and it's horrible. When the coffins were dug up in the churchyard one of them wasn't there."

"Arthur Snaithe told you that?"

She shuddered.

"It was my great grandmother's coffin. I

can't stop thinking about it."

"The county archivist will have all the records. Do you want me to find out more about it?"

"Please, David, no. I can't bear to know any more. I wish I'd never started all this."

David grunted and turned away to pick another piece of grass, and she didn't know whether he agreed with her or not. She had made a terrible mistake. She should bury the past, forget it, and concentrate on the present. She gazed down at the river which looked shadowy and remote to her now as it wound its way between the trees.

"Don't look so sad," David said turning back to her and smiling. "It's all right for you. Think of me slogging away on the Craven Walk tomorrow."

Back to that again. Perhaps it was just as well.

As they stood up he made a sudden move towards her. Surprised, she hesitated and the next moment was in his arms. He smelled faintly of crushed grass as he held her close.

"No, David, no! This is wrong."

She pulled away from him, her face flaming. Immediately he released her. He looked perplexed and hurt, but she couldn't help it. She had to make him understand. She had thought they were friends, not that he would begin to think there could ever be anything else between them.

"Please, David."

"There's someone else?"

"Yes, no. David, I can't."

"There's someone else?"

She turned away, hating herself.

"I can't explain."

But she must try. David had gone out of his way to help her, to find things out for her and to take her to see the place she most wanted to see. She was grateful, but that was all it could ever be.

"Maybe it's too soon," he said. "I should have waited."

She turned back to him.

"No, no. It's no use, David. I'm sorry."

He looked at her strangely for a moment. Then he took her hand and they began to go down the hill together to the river path. He said nothing more as they walked back along the path to the town. But he looked perplexed and downcast.

The sky was a mass of lowering grey as Rachel took up her position at the table near the front of the house next morning. She looked anxiously at the clouds. David had told her they could cope with anything, but the ground would be slippery and the becks icy cold.

Later she had promised to go down to Rawthwaite with Julie and help get everything ready for the evening get-together. Mrs Woodfield, looking better this morning, would be out later to see how she was getting on at her post.

There were shouts, and the sound of feet on gravel. Rachel jotted down the numbers on the disks the men held out to her. No sooner had they gone than more people arrived, and she was kept so busy she found an hour had passed. Using the disks was a good idea, she thought. If anything happened and someone went missing people would know where the disk had been checked. Rachel shivered. Simon had told her about a man drowning in the slime of Flitstone Bog. In her mind she suddenly heard his voice teasing her with his talk of hobgoblins and telling her how his home, High Hob, got its name.

There was more activity after that, but the last of the participants didn't arrive until much later.

After being out in the fresh air most of the day Rachel felt her eyelids begin to droop when she and Julie got down to the hall in Rawthwaite with their boxes of goodies Julie had prepared. Ken from the Outdoor Shop came soon after, and then there was a rush of people all bright-eyed and tanned. The food looked good spread out on the tables. There were huge piles of filled rolls, meat pies, salads. The heavy aroma rising from the tureens of soup Julie carried in made Rachel's eyes water.

The outside door clattered. A man came running into the hall, his jeans covered in mud.

"There's been an accident," he cried.

Then he spoke quietly to Ken who turned to face the girls. He moved his lips, but no sound came out.

"It's Brian," Julie shrieked. "Where's Brian?"

"Aye," the man gasped out, "and David, up in Shutt Hob. The ambulance is there. It'll be on its way to hospital by now."

Rachel gripped the edge of the table. Beside her Julie made little moaning noises.

"I'll drive you, Julie," Ken said. "Rachel, too. Come on."

Afterwards Rachel wondered how she had managed to keep outwardly calm on the long drive to the hospital when inside she was a turmoil of panic that made her dizzy. The wide hospital door stood open like a giant trap. They were given cups of tea as they waited, and then Julie was called away. When she had gone Rachel sat still, thinking of nothing, until she was conscious that Ken was standing in front of her.

"I'm to take you home now, Rachel," he said. "David's mum and dad are with him. We'll do no good here."

"Is he all right?" she whispered, standing up.

"Aye, lass, he'll do. Brian, too. Julie's going to stay with him, but you and I'll get gone."

She allowed herself to be led out to Ken's car, not daring to think what might happen if David had hurt himself badly. Arriving at last at Alderbeck House, Mrs Woodfield met them in the hall, and took charge. Strong, sweet tea was produced and Ken made to drink some before he left. No-one spoke of the cause of the accident, or what David and Brian were doing in Shutt Hob Gorge which wasn't on the route of the Craven Walk.

"Julie's just phoned," Mrs Woodfield said. "She'll be home tomorrow, Brian, too. He's being kept in for observation. A sprained wrist, that's all, so they say. But we'll see."

The hot tea slid down Rachel's throat. She looked up bleakly.

"Come now," Mrs Woodfield said briskly.

"Bed for you, Rachel."

She had no recollection of how she got there, only of raucous violin music coming from the sitting-room as they passed. She had a sudden vision of David running towards her in his blue jersey and brown cords as she sat at the checkpoint table only hours before.

Even after Mrs Woodfield rang the hospital and was told that David was going to be all right, Rachel couldn't settle to anything next day. She tried phoning his home, but there was no answer. Then she tried the Outdoor Shop. Ken's voice, though reassuring, could only tell her what she already knew.

"It's a right mystery, lass," Ken said. "You'll have to ask Brian why they were there in the gorge when he gets back today. Tell him I'll be up to see him this evening. Aye, there's plenty to talk about."

She couldn't even get down to Rawthwaite to get David a get-well card because Nerissa had gone off to Harrogate in her mother's car. The best she could do was write him a quick letter and run down the lane to post it in the nearest postbox half a mile away. She walked slowly back up the hill, deep in thought. David had left the planned route yesterday, but why?

A car drew up beside her, Mrs Woodfield's car. Nerissa wound down the window from her side.

"Get in."

Rachel did as she was told. Nerissa, in her white jersey and skirt, looked younger today. The dark hair was tied back from her smiling face with a red ribbon. Nerissa smiling! What could have happened?

"I've just been to the post," Rachel said, feeling the need to explain herself. "I'm to do the ironing when I get back."

Nerissa put the car into gear.

"Ironing?" she said as they moved off. "That's Julie's job. Let her do it. You've got other things to do. The flowers in the sitting-room look messy. Get them sorted. And there's a letter to type."

"The flowers are done already," Rachel said quickly. "I promised I'd do the ironing today for Julie, and that's what I'm going to do. She's got today off because of Brian."

Nerissa's smile faded for a moment.

"Ah, yes, Brian. Home today so I've been told. This very afternoon. He looks his usual self."

"You've seen him?"

"And why not? But what's that to you?"

The glance Nerissa flashed her was a warning. Then she smiled again as if at some delightful secret. Rachel couldn't begin to think what it could mean. In any case they were arriving at the house now. The tyres crunched on the gravel, and she was reminded vividly of the feet that had pounded it only yesterday. Weeks seemed to have passed since she took her place at the table yesterday morning ready to mark off the participants of the Craven Walk as they came running towards her.

She went inside. Julie wasn't back yet from the hospital. The best thing she could do for her at the moment was to get the ironing out of the way, but first she checked that Mrs Woodfield didn't need her.

Back in the kitchen again she set to work. Deep in thought she moved the iron backwards and forwards across the pillowcase on the ironing board. Soon the blouses hanging on the back of a kitchen chair and the sweet-smelling cotton sheets on the table bore witness to her hard work, but all she could think about was the accident.

CHAPTER SEVEN

Rachel placed the iron on its stand as the kitchen door burst open and Julie rushed in.

"I'm back!" she cried.

Her untidy hair hung over her forehead as if she hadn't had any thought for herself for hours.

"Brian's home. We've just got back from hospital."

"That's great," Rachel said. "He's all right?"

Julie's broad face broke into a smile.

"He's grand. I've just come over to tell Mrs Woodfield."

"But, Julie, what about David? Have you seen David?"

"The doctor was going in to see him when we left. I know nowt else."

"You don't know when they'll let him come home?"

Julie shook her head sympathetically.

"I'll be back to talk in a minute, Rachel."

"Mrs Woodfield's in the sitting-room. She'll be pleased about Brian."

For a moment after Julie had gone out, the room began to spin. Rachel sat down hastily. She didn't expect David to be out of hospital already, but she couldn't help hoping. Then she got up again, unplugged the iron and placed the finished ironing in the ironing basket ready to be carried upstairs to the airing cupboard. She turned, smiling, as Julie, came back into the kitchen.

"Coffee?"

"I'll get straight back or Brian will be wondering. I'm to have the rest of the day off, tomorrow, too, if need be."

"Oh, Julie, why did it happen? What were they doing in Shutt Hob Gorge? Did Brian tell you?"

"Brian's told me nothing. He might tell you though, Rachel. Come back to the cottage with me now and talk to him."

Rachel hesitated. She glanced at the ironing basket. Julie looked at it, too, and smiled.

"Mrs Woodfield won't need you the rest of the afternoon. She said so just now. What's the harm?"

None at all, Rachel thought. With Julie there, too, what could happen? And she had to know. David being in Shutt Hob Gorge had something to do with her, and she couldn't bear not knowing.

"All right," she said. "Thanks."

Julie walked quickly, anxious to be home. They didn't speak. Rachel was too worried at what Brian might have to tell her, and Julie had plenty on her mind, too.

Somehow Rachel expected Brian to look different, but he looked at her in his usual brash way as Julie ushered her into the warm kitchen. He was sitting at the scrubbed table, a newspaper in his hands.

He put it down at once when he saw that his wife was not alone.

"Someone to see you, lad," Julie said. "Rachel's got plenty to ask you so mind you tell her the truth of it all."

Rachel flushed and stared hard at his bandaged wrist as Julie pulled out a chair for her to sit down. Brian grinned.

"You look right pale, lass. No harm done."

"What about David?"

"Tougher than he looks is David. It was right bad luck. He should have had more sense than land me in trouble as well as himself."

"But what happened?"

Brian leaned forward and held out his bandaged wrist towards her.

"I got this at David's bidding. Like a fool I went up the cliff after him and got this for my pains."

"What cliff?" Rachel cried.

"David reckoned he needed to get the feel of the gorge again while he was nearby as he was ahead of time. Don't ask me why. I thought he knew something about the route I hadn't been told, and I followed him. Then he started to climb up. A short cut, that's what he said and I was fool enough to believe him."

For a moment Rachel felt she was there in

the gorge with them, with the rock crumbling beneath her feet and the crash of the waterfall in the distance and the gloomy trees overhead. Then her vision cleared and she saw Brian's laughing eyes as he deliberately broke off what he was saying to tease her. He seemed to have some secret knowledge that amused him alone.

"Did he tell you why?"

"That I can't say."

Rachel stared hard at the silver rose bowl as if that could tell her what she wanted to know even if Brian wouldn't. Brian grinned triumphantly. His eyes followed hers.

"Aye, that's my mum's silver bowl. Have you seen it close up, lass? It's a rare beauty."

She cringed back as if he had struck her. His dark eyes danced at her.

"But you'll know that already, won't you?"

What did he mean? Did he know about their relationship after all? She gulped, looking away from him in case he saw the knowledge in her face. Had David . . . But David would never tell him, not in a thousand years. He knew it was a sacred secret.

"Aye, our great grandad was a silversmith, and a right good one, too. Yours and mine, Rachel, yours and mine."

She looked at him in horror and his taunting eyes laughed back at her. She sprang to her feet. She didn't wait for more but rushed away from the cottage to stand leaning on the churchyard gate. Her gasping breaths exhausted her so that she couldn't move for some moments. She knew David wouldn't tell Brian, not deliberately. Had Brian wormed it out of him somehow?

No way could she return to the house knowing that Brian knew that he and she were related. She needed to think, to come to terms with it somehow so that nothing showed on her face to worry Mrs Woodfield. Suddenly it was all too much. At the churchyard gate she paused with her hand on the latch. Then, determinedly, she pushed the gate open and marched to the church door. Inside would be peace and quiet. No-one would disturb her there. No-one would know where she was either, and at this moment that seemed the best thing of all.

Simon's Land-Rover was parked in the drive when she got back to the house. He was in the hall talking to Mrs Woodfield as Rachel came in. She took a deep breath and smiled, anxious to show that all was well even though it wasn't. Simon looked at her keenly as if he knew what had just happened. Disconcerted she looked away. There was a sound from the landing above and

Nerissa came downstairs still wearing the white jersey and skirt she had seen her in earlier.

"Is Mother ready to accompany you, Simon?" she asked.

She still had that secret smile lurking at the corners of her mouth. It was the same sort of smile Rachel had seen when Nerissa spoke of seeing Brian in hospital.

As soon as she could, Rachel escaped, and ran up to her room. They were a family, a proper family. They belonged together. There was no room for her here, a stranger. She had no more real part here than she had in the home of Mr and Mrs Felpham, and never would.

She threw herself down on the bed and let the tears come. She couldn't bear it any longer, seeing Simon with Nerissa, knowing now some of the anguish caused by Sarah and Harry. And knowing, too, that her wish had come true in a way she would never have imagined. She had found a relative of her own, Brian, but one she wished she had never met. She was no nearer discovering any other member of her grandmother's family.

After a while she sat up and wiped her eyes. She would go away from Alderbeck. How could she stay here now? Seeing Brian every day would be sheer torture. She would phone Mr Felpham immediately. She would find Mrs Woodfield and tell her what she had decided, and then telephone.

Unbidden, the view that first day from the top of the hill shot into her mind. Bleak stone walls on rough hillsides — how could she bear to leave it? And to leave Harry and Sarah, too, and any hope now of healing the guilt she herself felt because of what had happened in the past. How had her grandmother coped with leaving her home? But she had Harry who loved her. She, Rachel Paget, had no-one, only the knowledge that she was bound up in some inexplicable way with the events that had happened long ago.

Full of aching loneliness, Rachel went out into the garden to look for Mrs Woodfield. She found her working in the flowerbeds some way from the house, a pair of secateurs in one hand and dead daffodils in the other. She looked businesslike with the sleeves of her jersey rolled up to the elbow.

"A lot needs doing," she called, throwing the dead heads into a wicker basket at her feet. "My dear, what's wrong? David's going to be all right, isn't he?"

"I've written to him," Rachel said. "I wanted to see him urgently. You see, I have to go. I have to leave here."

"Go? But, my dear . . ."

Mrs Woodfield put down the secateurs, and motioned towards the garden seat beneath the cherry tree.

"Come and talk, and tell me what it's all about."

They sat down. For a moment Rachel looked at the bare branches above her head, and then across the grass to the hills rising into the grey sky beyond. She would never forget it, never lose the feeling of freedom and space she had learned to love and now must lose. She gave a little shiver.

"You've been kind, letting me stay on. But now you're better, I can't stay any longer."

Mrs Woodfield smiled.

"Not a bit of it. You've helped me a lot, Rachel. It's been a sad time with the worry about Nerissa as well. You've provided a new interest, my dear. I enjoyed the detective work at the museum and looking through all those old letters I'd forgotten about."

"That's just it," Rachel said miserably. "It's no good raking up the past. I don't want to do it any more. I'll do as Mr Felpham wants, and go back to London."

"You will? But, my dear . . ."

"You've been so kind," Rachel repeated and choked back the tears in her throat.

"But, you see, I have to leave here."

"If that's what you want, then you must go, my dear. It's your decision, but I'll be sorry to lose you. You've had a bad time, too, Rachel, seeing your aunt so ill, but now you can look to the future, and make a life for yourself."

Mrs Woodfield looked towards the house and smiled. Violin music seemed to ripple through the calm air, gently at first and then stronger as if the player was feeling her way into confidence and strength.

"Nerissa has got over it all remarkably well," she said. "In fact she looks happier now than I've seen her for a long time. Her music hasn't suffered."

She broke off, as if there was something she wanted to say but was unable to form into words.

"It's Julie I'm worried about now," she said instead.

"Julie?"

"She hasn't seemed herself for a while."

They were both silent. Rachel remembered the way Julie was always so angry at Nerissa. She had known them both such a little time she was unable to judge how it had been before. Now she would never know.

"I'm grateful to you, Rachel. You've been

good for me, and for Julie, too. She likes having you here. But of course you must go if that's what you want. We mustn't stand in your way. You're not worried about not being able to discover anything more about your grandparents?"

Rachel shook her head. It was impossible to explain the dreary misery of it all. She had to go away and try to forget. Underneath everything was a lot you could never understand properly however hard you tried. She hadn't told anyone about her grandfather and Rose, and how this connected her with Brian. Only David knew. And now she wished she hadn't told him. If she stayed here, the painful knowledge would be with her all the time, haunting her.

"I'd like to phone Mr Felpham if I may."

"Of course, my dear. Do it now. Better still, why not go down to London on Monday and tell him face to face? Tell him that's what you'll do. Then come back for a day or two so you can visit David before you go for good."

"Could I?"

"Of course, my dear. We'll arrange for a taxi to get you to Harrogate. That's no problem. And to meet you on your return, too. I think I owe you that, Rachel."

On Monday, Rachel was up early, dressed in a dark skirt and sweatshirt, and with her thick dark hair tied back from her face. She clutched her rucksack, empty apart from her purse, having no other suitable bag with her.

Half past twelve, Mr Felpham had said, at his office in London. They would have lunch at a nearby restaurant and then spend the rest of the afternoon at home where Mrs Felpham would be waiting for them.

She stood outside King's Cross station in brilliant sunshine. She was surprised how familiar it felt. Yorkshire seemed a million light years away. There was plenty of time to fill in. She would walk to Mr Felpham's office which wasn't far away. Mr Felpham looked older to her now than he had when he was her aunt's solicitor and friend. Looking at his greying hair Rachel felt older, too, than when she had last seen him only two weeks ago. So much had happened, so very much.

He greeted her warmly, but there was a sad look about his eyes that hadn't been there before. Was it from anxiety about her? She felt ashamed suddenly. It wasn't until they were seated in a small, dim room, where an elderly waitress in black and white hovered round for their order, that she was able to say how sorry she was for going off without warning. She tried to explain what she'd done.

"You see, the advertisement was in the paper and it seemed so right. I wanted to try something on my own, and I just went . . ."

She broke off, flushing, aware she sounded selfish and mean after all he and Mrs Felpham had done for her.

"I know, my dear, I know," he said kindly. "Youth has these sudden impulses. No harm done, and you found your feet with Mrs Woodfield. I could tell that as soon she telephoned. I can't deny it was a shock at first for both of us, but then we got thinking. We had no right to stand in your way if that's what you really wanted to do. Anyway we came to terms with it, and of course we had to. We couldn't insist on your staying here if your mind was made up. Your aunt wouldn't have wished that. And you have found your own feet to stand on in a place that sounds suitable. Mrs Felpham and I are glad for you, and wish you well."

Rachel looked at him in silence, remembering how Aunt Sophie had been tight-lipped about the past.

"Now, my dear, are you going to tell me why you have come today?"

"I wanted to see you both," Rachel said. "I need to talk."

He looked pleased, waited until a bowl of tomato soup was placed before him and then said kindly, "As you know, your aunt's house is in the hands of the estate agents, and her things will be put into store for you for the time being when the house is sold. As her executor I shall deal with it all. As your guardian and trustee there will be some money for your immediate needs, as well as some in trust for you for later."

She nodded, having heard all this before.

"And of course, you'll need to pack the rest of your things, won't you? We've looked after them carefully and placed them in two big boxes on the landing for when you come for them."

Surprised into silence, she drank her soup rather hot so that a burning feeling slid down inside her. He was anxious to know what Mrs Woodfield was like, and how Rachel liked living in such a lonely place. As she told him something of how it had been, she couldn't help a certain enthusiasm coming into her voice. He smiled.

"We're so pleased for you, Rachel."

She glanced round the room. There was the chink of cutlery and the subdued murmur of voices. The scent from the hyacinths

118

that wafted across from the sideboard against the wall reminded her of Julie's cottage. A picture of the lane into Rawthwaite came into her mind, and for an instant she wondered what she was doing here.

"I have some papers that might interest you, my dear," he said. "Some copies of old certificates and such like."

"Thank you," she said, but it was too late.

She wasn't interested any more in knowing when Harry had married Sarah, or even if he hadn't. Old, painful things needed to stay in the past. For the rest of the meal she told him about the Craven Walk, and the lively get-together planned for that evening that had been cut short for herself and Julie.

"It's David, you see," she said hesitantly. "He's a friend. He had an accident. The hospital's thirty miles away, but he'll be home soon."

She couldn't go away without seeing David. It was only fair to hear his side of what had happened. She had to see him. But why had the Felphams placed her belongings in boxes?

In the bustle of finishing the meal and getting out of the restaurant, there wasn't the opportunity to ask why, but she understood when they arrived at the house and Mrs

Felpham came forward to greet her. She was wearing the same green dress as usual and her greying hair was pulled back into the same hairstyle. What was different was the elderly lady seated by the fire in the living-room, looking very much at home.

"My mother," Mr Felpham said. "Mama, this is Rachel, our ward, come to see us for the day."

Rachel smiled, and shook hands, feeling suddenly lost. Didn't they want her any more? Now was the moment to ask, but she let it pass. Then it was too late because Mrs Felpham was saying, proudly, that they had plans to change her old room into a bed-sitting-room for her mother-in-law.

There was only one thing to do when Mr Felpham drove her to the station in time for the early evening train. Some of the money he had given her would be put to good use right away at left luggage, where the large suitcase he had lent her would be deposited until she could collect it in a few days' time. She could hardly arrive at Alderbeck House with it when Mrs Woodfield knew her mind was made up about going!

Mrs Woodfield took one look at Rachel's pale face and sent her off to bed. It was impossible to remonstrate, to say that the last thing she wanted was to lie awake for hours going over and over in her mind the reception that she had received at Mr and Mrs Felpham's.

No prizes for guessing what would happen if she told Mrs Woodfield. She would immediately take pity on her and insist she stay on here. But she didn't want that. How could she stay on at Alderbeck, knowing there was no real job here for her any more? She had more pride than that. No, she must work something out for herself, as she had done before when she had decided to apply for the job here in the first place.

Rachel woke, unrefreshed, next morning with the problem still unsolved. There had been a phone message from David while she was in London which Mrs Woodfield had told her about as soon as she got back. He was home from hospital, but had to take it easy for a day or two and he'd be in touch.

Since she wasn't needed in the house until later she would go for a walk to kill some time until she could contact David. Why not go to Shutt Hob Gorge? She wanted to see it once more before she left Alderbeck. It was something to do.

After breakfast she pulled on her jacket and went downstairs. To her surprise Nerissa was in the hall talking to Brian. She seemed to sparkle at him. Brian, in a red tartan shirt, leaned against the banisters looking for all the world as if he was the master here. Nerissa turned to look at Rachel, her dark eyes gleaming.

"The little spy!"

Rachel felt herself flush.

"So?" Nerissa drawled. "Off out, are we? Why the hurry?"

"Only for a walk," Rachel said pausing awkwardly. "Not far."

Nerissa shrugged, no longer interested, but Brian looked at her closely.

"The weather's worsening, lass."

"But it's all right now. It doesn't take long to reach Sh . . ."

Rachel paused, confused, aware that she had nearly let out where she was going. Not that either would care where she went. They were too interested in their own conversation for that. She heard the murmur of their voices as she shut the door behind her, but forgot them immediately as she ran across the gravel to the gate into the churchyard. Today she didn't linger to look at tombstones, but hurried into the lane and scuttled past Julie's cottage in case she was seen and delayed.

She arrived, breathless, at the mouth of the gorge and followed the path to where the water forced itself over the cliff and fell to the beck beneath. Today it seemed gloomy instead of spectacular as it had done the first time David had brought her here. Then she had been interested. Now, she knew it for a tragic place. She gazed up at the trees overhanging the limestone. With a shimmer of apprehension she saw that it wasn't the tree alone that shaded the light. Clouds covered the sky, and in the distance came a low rumble. Thunder?

The storm came unbelievably fast. Huge raindrops stung her face as she started to run back the way she had come. The path was thick with mud. A crack of thunder echoed among the cliffs like a roll of drums and had hardly faded away before another blinding flash of lightning made her gasp and run for shelter in an indent in the cliff where she stood huddled.

A low sound make her tilt her head to listen. A human voice in all this tumult? But there was only the lash of rain on the bare rock above her head. Then came the simultaneous flash and crash.

She cringed back, her hand over her eyes. As the roaring faded she heard the shout again.

"Here, I'm over here!" she cried.

Someone was there, and she was thankful

not to be alone. Then she caught a glimpse of red among the trees and knew at once who he was. Too late to do anything but wait to be found. He came crashing towards her, his voice deep with relief.

"Brian!" she cried, trying to control the hysterical note in her own voice.

"There you are, lass. I thought you'd been struck."

He reached her in a few long strides. Water poured from his dark head, and his red shirt stuck to his body.

"By, lass, you chose a good time to come here."

The rain was easing off now, and the thunder rumbled away into the distance. Water still dripped from the trees, and the ground beneath her feet was awash. She felt ashamed at her panic, and wished she hadn't called out and drawn his attention to her presence.

"But what happened?"

He wiped his arm across his face, and then stopped abruptly and stared in awe.

"Look behind you."

She sprang round and gazed open-mouthed at the great fissure that yawned in the rock as if someone had sliced it with a giant knife. Brian's back tensed as he pushed past her and hauled himself up to peer inside.

"What is it?" she asked anxiously.

He leaned farther across, and she thought suddenly of David's accident.

"Be careful!"

He was almost inside, but he wriggled free and jumped down beside her. She saw that his face shone with excitement and there was a wild look in his eyes. Hastily she jumped down on to the path.

"What's in there? What have you seen, Brian?"

He gave a shout of laughter.

"Wouldn't you like to know, little cousin?"

Now he seemed threatening as he moved towards her. Instantly she took off, leaping through the trees on to the track. Slithering along, she could think only of that first time he had crept up on her in the churchyard, frightening her out of her wits. She knew he would catch her. There was no hope that he wouldn't. His pounding footsteps thundered behind her. Then he caught hold of her arm and yanked her to a stop.

"I like a lass with spirit," he said.

She struggled and called out, "Let me go!"

He let go of her suddenly, the laughter fading from his swarthy face. The rain sluiced down on them.

"Come on, lass, run for it before we both

drown."

Rachel's mind cleared suddenly as she turned and ran. She was gasping as they pelted through the churchyard and along the path to the house. At the door he caught hold of her again and slewed her round to face him.

"Treated David badly by all accounts, didn't you, lass? No wonder he was careless of his life. Mine, too. You've a debt to pay."

She stiffened and glared back at him.

"It's none of your business. So let me go and get out of my way. A stirrer, that's you, Brian. There's nothing between David and me and I don't believe he said there was."

She shook herself free, conscious of the open door and of Simon standing there. He moved swiftly aside to let her pass.

"Rachel, my dear!" Mrs Woodfield cried as Rachel staggered, dripping wet, through the hall and into the kitchen.

"I'm sorry," Rachel gasped. "I didn't mean . . ."

"Did Brian find you? I sent him after you."

Tears sprang into Rachel's eyes, and she gulped. She saw Mrs Woodfield through a blur and then saw that Simon was there, too. He pulled forward a chair. She sank down on it, hardly conscious of what she was doing.

"She must get into dry clothes before she gets a chill," Mrs Woodfield's anxious voice came.

"Brandy first. She's had a shock."

A glass was put to her lips, and she took a sip. The warm glow slid down her throat so unexpectedly she spluttered. The glass was taken from her, and she heard Julie's deep voice as she was helped upstairs.

"I'll run the shower, Rachel. Hand me out them wet clothes when you're ready. I'll find my towelling robe for you to put on."

She could hear Julie moving about in the bedroom as she turned off the water and wrapped a bath towel round herself to go to the door to take the robe Julie had ready.

"Aye, you've had a right bad shock," Julie said sympathetically as Rachel emerged. "The storm coming so quick, and you in that place."

Rachel started to towel her hair.

"What place?"

"It were Brian who knew where you'd gone. Shutt Hob Gorge, under all them trees in a thunderstorm. A wonder you weren't struck."

Rachel stared at her.

"Of course, Brian!"

"Brian? Has he done ow't?"

Julie's voice sounded strange. Suddenly

Rachel thought of the papers Mr Felpham had given her. Where were they now? Thrust hurriedly into her top drawer? Why should she think of them now anyway when they were no longer important to her? She continued to towel her damp hair, thankful to be indoors.

To her surprise Rachel slept well that night. When she woke and looked at her watch and saw it was seven o'clock she got out of bed. Reaching for her clothes she dressed hurriedly, not wanting to waste a moment of the precious time she had left. Then she began to rummage among her things in her top drawer, impatient to find what she had thought of so suddenly when she got back soaked to the skin yesterday.

Here it was, the envelope Mr Felpham had given her. With shaking fingers she pulled out the contents and scattered them on the bed. There were some old bills, for clothes mostly, and the birth certificate of one Ellen Sophie. Robert Haddon, textile merchant, was her father, and her mother was Jane. Rachel smoothed the paper, and gazed in awe. Such a long time ago! Who was Ellen Sophie? Could she be Sarah Swinbank's mother, her own great grandmother? Quickly she worked it out. If her mother had waited till thirty to have her baby the dates fitted for that baby to have been this Ellen Sophie.

She paused, marvelling. Incredible that this had turned up now. If only she had been given this with the diary before she came North how valuable it would have been! Proof positive that the family she had come to seek had actually existed. She took one last look and folded it carefully.

Then she saw that there was something else, too. It was part of an old letter, faded now after all this time. With trembling fingers Rachel opened it out and stared at the thin writing. The letter was from someone called James Thirgood, solicitor. A headstone was mentioned. The blood rushed to her face. But there was no further mention of any name, only that the headstone had been placed as instructed against the wall of St Michael's Church, Alderbeck, their own church. She looked for a date on the letter, but found none because the top of the letter where the date would have been was torn off as if someone didn't want the address of James Thirgood, solicitor, to be kept.

Why hadn't she seen the headstone when she went searching that first morning?

She sat back on the bed, and tried to think. In her mind a picture formed of broken headstones leaning drunkenly in the long grass, and a tottering one that Brian said was his grandad's tomb with others nearby leaning against the wall of the church. She had examined them all, hadn't she?

Suddenly it was important to make sure. With Brian out of the way in Manchester today this was her chance. But first there were all the papers to put away safely in her top drawer. She gathered them together and slipped them inside the envelope to examine again later. The important thing now was to check about the headstone for her own peace of mind.

As she let herself out of the front door she saw Nerissa, dressed in a black suit and with her dark hair piled on top of her head.

"I'm taking Mother's car," she threw back over her shoulder. "Tell her, will you?"

She opened the boot, lifted two suitcases inside and then slammed it shut. Before Rachel could say anything she swung herself into the driver's seat, started the engine and drove off in a swirl of gravel.

A cold wind brushed against Rachel's cheeks as she gazed down at the yellowing lichen-covered headstone that leaned against the wall of the church as if it had no strength left after its removal here all those years ago. She shivered, wishing she had worn her jacket in her haste to get out of the house.

She could see now why she hadn't recognised the headstone before. The name Swinbank had been erased by time. The rest of the lettering was there, though, for anyone who knew. Ellen Sophie, nee Haddon, who died before Aunt Sophie was born. That much could be deciphered beneath the lichen when she looked hard. But what difference could it make to her now? Tears stung her eyes, and a weight of misery lay on her heart because it meant nothing to her after all. She would go away, and that would be the end of it.

She thought of Rose, poor, neglected Rose. Her son, Zachary, had grown up wild and selfish, and his daughter was Brian's grandmother. It was frightening how things worked out. The sad events of the past were like those of today. She, Sarah Swinbank's granddaughter, had imagined herself unravelling all sorts of interesting facts about the young girl who had run away with the silver engraver from Rawthwaite. She felt years older now than when she had travelled North to do just that with the precious diary in her rucksack and all her hopes intact.

A sudden shadow on the grass made her

heart beat wildly. She sprang round. Simon stood looking at her gravely.

"Sorry to startle you, Rachel," he said. "Mrs Woodfield sent me to find you."

His mouth looked tight in his tanned face, and his eyes were hard.

"Is something wrong?"

"You're needed back at the house, Rachel, at once. It's Julie. She's in a state of shock."

"I only came out for a moment. Look, I've found my great grandmother's headstone. They put it here when they flooded the graveyard under Garth Scar. Do you think they put her coffin here, too? I thought Brian had found it in the gorge."

She heard herself prattling on, unable to stop. It was something to do with the way Simon looked as he stood in the long grass in his rough working clothes, so different from the Simon she knew, or thought she knew.

His face darkened as he spoke, "Nerissa's left Alderbeck for good. So has Brian."

For a moment she was unable to take it in. She stared back at him.

"Not Brian and Nerissa together? She can't have, not Nerissa."

"Aye. The truth's out at last. He's always been after her."

Rachel gazed at him, appalled. She put

out a hand to the tombstone to steady herself.

"Oh, poor Julie!"

She thought of Harry and Sarah with painful urgency. It was the same thing happening again. Suddenly Simon turned to go, and she went with him, hurrying across the grass to keep up with his long strides.

"Of course the coffin was re-interred here," he called back to her as they reached the path. "Remember that Brian can't be trusted further than you can see him, especially now, after this. Your help is needed with Julie. Come on, Rachel. Hurry, lass."

Once through the churchyard gate his pace quickened and Rachel ran to keep up with him. She followed him into the kitchen at a rush, slamming the door shut behind her. Julie's jacket lay on the floor where she had dropped it when she had come stumbling in to tell her employer the news she had only just discovered for herself. Julie's face was blotched and puffy, and her creased white blouse hung out of her skirt.

"Make her a hot drink, Rachel," Mrs Woodfield said. "She'd better stay here at the house for the time being."

"He didn't saw owt," Julie cried. "I wasn't to know. And now he's gone."

She fell into a fit of crying as Rachel put her arms round her and held her tight. Julie broke away.

"I'll not stay at Alderbeck. I'll go to my aunt in Leeds. I can't stay here, I can't."

"I'll give the doctor a ring," Simon said grimly. "We can't have you knocking yourself up, Celia."

Mrs Woodfield's face was pale, but she held herself upright as if she was not going to let this sudden blow get her down.

"Rachel's here," Mrs Woodfield said. "We'll manage. Rachel, my dear, could you make up a bed for poor Julie in the room next to mine? We'll get her upstairs now. Simon, could you help?"

Rachel jumped up from her kneeling position on the floor. Julie now sat slumped with her elbows on the table and her head in her hands. The hot chocolate Rachel had made for her was untouched. Together Rachel and Simon got Julie upstairs to the spare room. While she was making up the bed and getting Julie to lie down Simon made coffee downstairs for the rest of them.

"Is she asleep?" Mrs Woodfield asked as Rachel went back to the kitchen.

She nodded, feeling drained. The hot drink was welcome.

"I'm hungry," she said. "I'll make some toast."

Simon looked anxiously at Mrs Woodfield.

"You've had a shock, too, Celia. You need to rest as well as Julie. Rachel won't mind looking after herself."

Rachel placed two slices of bread in the toaster. She knew what he meant. She had no part in this family crisis. She didn't belong. He had no need to spell it out.

"I'm so sorry you're plunged into all this, Rachel my dear," Mrs Woodfield said. "Take some time off for yourself this morning while Julie's sleeping. I'd like to be alone in my room. There's nothing you can do at the moment."

Or at any other time, Rachel thought as Mrs Woodfield went out of the room. Her usefulness here had gone, especially if Julie did as she said and left Alderbeck, too. She had no part in Alderbeck. She didn't belong.

Simon drained his cup.

"There's work to be done, Nerissa or no Nerissa. I suppose I've always felt responsible for Brian because we are distantly related. We hoped he'd settle down when he married Julie. Obviously he hasn't, and now there's all this mess."

"Brian's related to me as well," Rachel whispered.

"I'm not blaming you."

"I should think not," Rachel cried. "This is nothing to do with me, nothing!"

She broke off, confused. Why was she shouting at Simon? He was part of the set-up here because he was once married to Nerissa. He belonged, and she didn't. He seemed not to have heard what she said.

"Rain won't be long in coming again," he said. "I can smell it on the air. Arthur Snaithe reckons the reservoirs have never been as low since the valleys were flooded."

"So the church tower and the ruined house, they'll be sticking up out of the water now?"

"Aye, they will that. The first time for years, with the water so low even after the heavy rain yesterday."

She stared at Simon. At the back of her mind was the suspicion that all the bad things that happened in the past resulted from the young Sarah Swinbank, her grandmother. All the time sad things went round in circles for ever. She couldn't cope with it any more.

Grabbing Julie's jacket from the floor she thrust her arms into the armholes.

"I'm going to see for myself," she cried.

"No, lass, wait!"

"I can't wait."

136

Hardly knowing what she thought or believed, Rachel rushed to the door.

Chapter Eight

The rain hadn't come yet, but the sky was grey and lowering. Rachel ran through the garden at the back of the house, and up the hillside to reach the track she had followed that first morning when she had escaped from the kitchen because Brian was there with Julie. So long ago, it seemed. So much had happened since then.

A curlew sent out its high, wild call as Rachel pushed her way up through the dry heather to the summit. She had a long way to go yet, so she didn't linger. She didn't dare. If once she stopped she would realise the difficulty of crossing the wild fell. She was gasping as she ran down the other side and began clambering again. After a while she slowed down a little as the old heather stalks bit into her ankles. The long, faded grass hid sudden potholes in the uneven ground and she had to be careful or she would have tripped and fallen headlong.

At last she topped the last skyline. On the other side was Garth Scar reservoir. At first she was afraid to look down for what she might see there. Instead she raised her eyes to the hills near Shutt Hob Gorge that looked misty in the far distance. As she watched they seemed to disappear into the low cloud until she could see them no more.

She needed to know, she had to know what the church tower looked like beneath the water, but it was the hardest thing in the world to look down to the calm grey sheet of water. Very slowly, with her breath held, she let her gaze travel down the hillside and out across the water. Something glimmered darkly — a shadow, several dark shadows. She let out her breath, her heart pounding

Dark shapes showed beneath the water, and something that stuck up like a rock. Part of the church? She stared. This had lain hidden for fifty years, and she was able to see it now. A feeling of awe crept up her throat. She had thought it would be frightening but instead deep relief stole over her. It was interesting and awe-inspiring, that was all.

She could hardly stop looking, but she was too far away here on the top of the hill. She must get nearer, down to the water's edge to have a really good look. She ran down the rough hillside to where the banks of the reservoir were dotted with boulders and patches of gravel. She stared out at the reservoir, disappointed. Down here on a level with the water she could see nothing except the single rock-like tip of the church.

She raised her eyes to the surrounding hills, and tried to imagine how it had been before the water came. Much the same as today, apart from the buildings. Her young grandmother would have looked at the same hills, have listened to the sheep and the curlews and seen the rabbits cropping the grass. And then Harry Brent had come and swept her off her feet.

When she had first read about it in the pages of the diary her young grandparents' flight had seemed like a romantic story, but she knew the truth behind it now. She knew, too, that you had to understand about the unhappy things as well. The world wasn't a perfect place, then or now. A picture of Simon came into her mind with a suddenness that shook her. She saw him in the yard at High Hob in his working clothes. His boots had been clogged with mud. As he looked at her the wrinkles round his eyes deepened as he gave her the slow smile she had come to know and love. She would never forget him.

She was glad she had come to Alderbeck House in spite of everything. Sighing, she began to walk up the hill, pausing halfway to look back at the reservoir. The dark shadows were visible again now that she could see it in perspective. When she was miles away from here she would see her life here in perspective, too.

Rain began to fall with a thin veiling of mist against her face. She walked on towards the barn. Turning again, she saw that the water was blotted out now. Low cloud swirled round her, getting thicker by the minute. The top of the hill had vanished and so had the barn that only a moment ago she had seen lower down on the hillside. The penetrating silence was frightening.

She turned round and tried to walk in a straight line down the hillside the way she had come earlier. But which was the way? It was impossible to tell. She turned round again, to try to locate the barn in the whiteness that swirled round her like ghostly hands. A sob rose in her throat. Suppose she stumbled and tripped, suppose she couldn't get up again?

She forced herself to stand still, to summon all the willpower she possessed to fight her panic. Then, taking a deep breath and letting it out slowly she moved forward. Her foot caught in a heather root but as she pulled it free she overbalanced and slid to the ground. The wet heather was soft to fall on, and she was already so wet that staying here didn't seem to matter. She could use a rest for a little while before she struggled again to find the route down.

She lay back and closed her eyes, feeling the clammy mist swirl round her. The silent, penetrating drizzle was heavier now, but it made no difference because she was already wet through. She pushed back her bedraggled hair, opened her eyes and sat up. Was the cloud a little higher now? She couldn't be sure.

She no longer felt even the merest spasm of fear. Marvelling, she thought back to her first glimpse of the church tower in the water and the ruins of Alderbeck Court — part of her heritage because of Sarah Swinbank. It was nothing to do with Brian because his great-grandmother was Rose, not Sarah whose home it was. She didn't have to go away. Brian had left, and Nerissa, too. They had gone away together, repeating the pattern of long ago.

She would soon have money of her own because of Aunt Sophie. She could stay here with Mrs Woodfield and contribute to the household instead of being a paid companion. At least she could make the suggestion. Somehow she felt it was the right one and that Mrs Woodfield would welcome it.

She stood up. The mist was beginning to clear lower down, but the rain still fell. She heard a shout.

"Rachel, are you there?"

A dog barked. Surprised, she stood and listened and heard it again. Fly bounded up to her, panting and delighted, and then Simon was there, too, bulky in his jacket. She felt an overwhelming relief that he was here. She slithered down to him.

"Simon, oh, Simon!"

"All right, lass?"

She looked at him, and those simple words were enough. He gazed down at her with such love she could hardly bear it. She raised her face in wonder. He stepped forward and the next moment she was in his arms with his deep voice murmuring his anguish and fear that he would never find her among these desolate fells. Then he kissed her long and hard.

She was breathless when he released her at last.

"Oh, Simon, I'm glad you came."

"Your young friend telephoned. Aye, David. I guessed where you had gone when he said he'd shown you Garth Scar. He told me how it was between you, too. I didn't know. He's a young lad more your age."

"A friend," she whispered. "Never more

than that. There was nothing between David and me."

"Aye, I know that now, Rachel. He'll be at the house when I get you back. He knows why I had to come."

She clasped his hands and raised them to her lips. For a second he stood still. Then he pulled her into his arms again. This time his kiss was gentle and she didn't want it to end. When at last he released her he gazed at her with the same loving look in his eyes.

"I'm too old for you. Do you know that, Rachel?"

She laughed shakily.

"Age, what does age matter?"

"A few years, that's all. You're right, lass. It doesn't matter. And now we need to get back before the weather worsens."

"I've got something I need to do first," she said urgently. "I saw them, the buildings underneath the water. Now I want to touch the barn, just one more time. I need to do it, Simon."

"We'll wait here, Fly and me. We'll not go anywhere without you."

She ran to the old building that loomed up large on the misty hillside in front of her, and put out a hand to touch it. Nothing happened.

"It's cold," she cried.

David had said stone could act as a conductor, that the emotions felt at Alderbeck Garth when Sarah and Harry fled were so strong they left impressions on the stone. So what did this mean now? That the emotions had faded, were at peace? That her own feelings about her grandparents had changed, and she herself had changed, too? She turned to go, and immediately there came to her a strange feeling of peace. She ran back to Simon.

"Rachel?"

She heard the anxiety in his voice as he came towards her.

"You look different, lass," he said in wonder.

"I am different. I can see more clearly now."

He smiled and held out his hand to her.

"The cloud's lifting."

Rachel looked round with delight as the grey curtain rolled back from the distant hills. It wasn't what she meant, but it could wait for the moment. Simon's face was pale, and the lines round his eyes were edged deep. She had caused him worry and she was sorry.

"I shan't let you go away ever again, Rachel, my love," Simon said. "You're needed here. Julie won't stay long with her aunt in

Leeds. When she gets over this she'll want to come back. You're needed at Alderbeck, lass."

Because of Brian, Julie could be counted as her relation, too, as well as Simon. Here was the family she had prayed for! She had no need to worry any more about belonging.

"And you, Simon, what about you? Do you need me?"

He caught hold of her arm and pulled her close. How could she doubt for a single moment his need of her? Rachel smiled, too, as she felt his arm go round her. They set off down the track together to the place she would always now call home.

We hope you have enjoyed this Large Print book. Other Thorndike, Wheeler, and Chivers Press Large Print books are available at your library or directly from the publishers.

For information about current and upcoming titles, please call or write, without obligation, to:

Publisher
Thorndike Press
295 Kennedy Memorial Drive
Waterville, ME 04901
Tel. (800) 223-1244

or visit our Web site at:

http://gale.cengage.com/thorndike

OR

Chivers Large Print
published by BBC Audiobooks Ltd
St James House, The Square
Lower Bristol Road
Bath BA2 3SB
England
Tel. +44(0) 800 136919
email: bbcaudiobooks@bbc.co.uk
www.bbcaudiobooks.co.uk

All our Large Print titles are designed for easy reading, and all our books are made to last.